20th J. 113.

THE TOW

Gyan Prakash is the Dayton
Princeton University. He is th
the acclaimed *Mumbai Fables*

Dear Akshatha
Have a gr8
read.

Luv
Pravin + Roopa
+ Mohit

THE TOWER OF SILENCE

PHIROSHAW JAMSETJEE CHEVALIER 'CHAIWALA'

Edited and with an introduction by
Gyan Prakash

HarperCollins *Publishers* India

First published in 2013 by
HarperCollins *Publishers* India

Copyright for this edition © Gyan Prakash 2013

ISBN: 978-93-5029-637-0

2 4 6 8 10 9 7 5 3 1

HarperCollins *Publishers*
A-53, Sector 57, Noida, Uttar Pradesh 201301, India
77-85 Fulham Palace Road, London W6 8JB, United Kingdom
Hazelton Lanes, 55 Avenue Road, Suite 2900, Toronto, Ontario M5R 3L2
and 1995 Markham Road, Scarborough, Ontario M1B 5M8, Canada
25 Ryde Road, Pymble, Sydney, NSW 2073, Australia
31 View Road, Glenfield, Auckland 10, New Zealand
10 East 53rd Street, New York NY 10022, USA

Typeset in 12/15 Baskerville
by Jojy Philip, New Delhi 110 015

Printed and bound at
Manipal Technologies Ltd, Manipal

LOOKING FOR MR CHAIWALA

Gyan Prakash

The publication of *The Tower of Silence*, more than eighty-five years after it was penned by Mr Chaiwala, is a happy moment. Certainly, the author would have been pleased to see his rollicking novel in print.

I first encountered Phirozeshah Jamsetjee Chaiwala in the British Library, London in 2001. I was in the initial stages of research for my book, *Mumbai Fables*, wading through some documents from the 1920s. Reading the dry, official correspondence, I silently cursed the British Raj. As if ruling India was not bad enough, it had also condemned historians to struggle through the records of its tedious routines of government. Trawling through reams of documents to pick up bits of information about the past is a historian's occupational hazard, but did the material have to be so dreary? I needed a break. Setting aside the stack of files on my desk, I began looking through the catalogue of the Oriental and India Office Collection's European manuscripts for some light entertainment. My eyes glazed over as they moved from listing to listing, from the letters and diaries of this Governor-General to the private correspondence and papers of that Viceroy. Suddenly, an entry for the *Tower of Silence* caught my eye. The catalogue described it as the typescript of a novel written in 1927. I immediately requisitioned it.

To my delight, when the typescript arrived, I discovered it was a detective novel. I put aside everything else and delved into it. Though I was not sure how it contributed to my research on Bombay, I was hooked. Here was something that matched the enchantment that the city held for me. The action was non-stop, full of twists and turns and, although it moved from place to place, Bombay was at its centre. For two straight days, I read nothing but *Tower of Silence*. But a disappointment awaited me. The typescript ended abruptly on page 169. It was clearly incomplete. Where was the rest?

In my pursuit of the concluding pages, I faced mystery after mystery. First, there was the author's name in the typescript: Phiroshaw Jamsetjee Chevalier (Chaiwala). It was clear enough that he was a Parsi. But Chevalier was not a Parsi last name. Chaiwala had obviously adopted it. But why? I consulted a Parsi friend who offered one possible explanation. He suggested that the author might have adopted the last name of Maurice Chevalier. Apparently the gramophone records of the French actor and singer were popular among the Parsis in the 1920s. This was plausible, though Chaiwala deepened the mystery of his adopted name by rubber-stamping the pages with the name of the publisher – P.J.

Chavalier and Co. – spelling the name with an 'a' rather than an 'e'.

But whether spelt with an 'a' or an 'e', there was no record of this company as a publisher. In fact, in *Thacker's India Directory* of 1927, it was listed as an export, import, and general commission agency with an office in Commissariat Building, Hornby Road, Bombay. Perhaps Chavalier & Co. decided to diversify its operations by entering publishing. But if it did, *Tower of Silence*, authored by the company's sole proprietor, was one of its two publications – the other being 'Sixty-Seven Poems', a hundred-page typescript also authored by Chaiwala.

Perhaps the sight of the publisher's stamp caused the India Office in London to deposit it in the printed books collection on 5 June 1930. The *Catalogue of Books Printed in the Bombay Presidency during the Quarter ending 30 September 1928* listed it as published on 15 May 1928, with a first edition consisting of 100 copies. It was transferred to the European manuscripts collection on 21 May 1976. Apparently the rubber stamp on the typescript no longer persuaded the library staff that the novel had been published. For Chaiwala, who must have believed the contrary, this would have been a terrible blow.

Who was Chaiwala? Or was it Chevalier or Chavalier? I gathered from reading his novel that he was a well-educated Parsi businessman from Bombay, fluent in English andwith literary ambitions. He took the trouble not only to self-publish his novel with a hundred typescript copies but also mailed one copy all the way to the India Office Library, London. But apparently only an incomplete version had reached its destination.

A further search in the British Library did not yield the missing pages, but I was convinced they existed. The methodical unfolding of the narrative, and the way the typescript was numbered and divided into chapters convinced me that Chaiwala was a careful man. It seemed unlikely that he had written and put into circulation an incomplete novel. Perhaps the missing pages of the India Office copy had gotten lost in the binding process, or come loose somewhere between the original filing in the printed books catalogue and later transfer to the manuscript collection. Where was it, then? I became obsessed with this question, and decided to locate the text.

THE HUNT

Both the man and the text posed mysteries. I did the only thing a historian could do, and made inquiries.

But first I asked a very efficient computer operator in Chennai to enter the typescript into a digital form. Latha did the job with amazing accuracy and promptness and mailed it to me with a comment: 'But sir, it appears the document is incomplete. What happens in the end?' While entering the typescript into the computer, the action-packed suspense drama had evidently captivated Latha. I promised that she would be the first to know when I found out and then I continued on to Mumbai.

I reasoned that since Chaiwala had taken the trouble to send his novel to the India Office in London, he must in all likelihood have also sent it to libraries in Mumbai. I scoured library after library, checking their catalogues and talking to the librarians. The search was time-consuming but full of unexpected delights. I gained a good knowledge of the collections in the city's libraries and how they were used and abused by their patrons. The conversation with librarians often moved from my particular query to general discourses on the city and the state of the Parsis.

One such conversation with Mr M, the librarian of one noted library named after a prominent Parsi philanthropist, was particularly memorable. After calling my search for Chaiwala's book noble, he began lamenting the state of his library. He alleged that patrons, particularly students, came to the library not to read books but for respite from the heat and to sleep under the fan in the reading room. He complained about the students but also expressed his sympathies. After all, most of the students came from modest backgrounds and lived in cramped spaces. He was happy to provide the library's cavernous and cool reading room as a place where they could relax and perhaps even do homework, but drew the line on eating lunch in the reading room, a rule, he said, that was frequently violated.

The violation of the reading room's rules became a prelude to a general discourse on the decline of order in the city. Mr M was an engineer by training and had agreed to become the librarian only because of a sense of duty to his community. But he said that even the Parsis were becoming lax. No one cared about rules and duties anymore in Mumbai. To prove his point, he proceeded to tell me about an incident at Cusrow Baug, a Parsi residential colony in Colaba. A resident in the colony refused to pay the common charges for trash collection because he claimed that his family generated no trash. Mr M was incredulous and told him that this was impossible in modern society. But the resident stuck to his claim. Suspecting that something was amiss, Mr M stood sentinel overnight. Sure enough, he spotted the suspected resident emerge under cover of darkness carrying a bagful of garbage. As he tried to hide his bag among those of other residents, Mr M caught his arm and said: 'Remember, I told you that you can not live in modern society and produce no trash.'

Mr M was not alone in lamenting the Parsis losing their way. As I searched the libraries and looked for Chaiwala's antecedents, I drew a blank but encountered a rich and contradictory discourse on the Parsi community. A well-dressed Parsi gentleman in Tardeo sat me down and launched into an extended speech on the past and present of the community. I had gone to Tardeo because an entry in the *Times of India Directory and Calendar* for 1927 listed Chaiwala as a resident of Bhiwandiwala House. When I asked someone on the street about the location of the building, he asked me who I was looking for. When I told him, he said: 'Oh, a Parsi from way back then? Yes, they were very important then. Look at them, now.' He pointed to an ill-kept building on Tardeo Road where lower middle-class Parsi women wearing faded dresses sat on the steps. When I approached the women with my questions about Chaiwala, none of them had heard of him and they assured me that no family with that name lived there. But they referred me to an elderly gentleman who stepped out of the building, telling me that he 'knew a lot about the past'.

The gentleman, dressed in a three-piece suit that had seen better days, was sweating in the October heat of Mumbai. But there was a dignity about him as he considered my question about Chaiwala. His family had lived in the building since the 1940s but he had never heard the name. 'A writer, you say. No, no such person could exist in this building today. If he ever did, he obviously had the good sense to leave.' With that, he proceeded to tell me about the glorious history of the Parsis. They had built the city. Look around, he said, and everywhere you will see buildings named after them and hospitals and colleges established by them. But now, it is all gone. The community had shrunk, slowly swallowed by everything around them.

I encountered similar elegiac sentiments in literature. There was an overwhelming sense of besiegement and disarray of the community in Rohinton Mistry's *Tales from Firozsha Baag* (1987), in Thrity Umrigar's *Bombay Time* (2002) and in many others. Tanya Luhrman's ethnographic study, *The Good Parsi* (1996) also finds conflicted feelings among the Parsis about the fate of their community in postcolonial India. On the one hand, there is a strong awareness of the fading memory of the community's distinct identity, history, and contributions to the city. On the other hand, there are contradictory sentiments about this loss. Some mourn that India has eaten into their once exalted position, forcing many to migrate to Australia, Canada, the UK, and the United States, rendering them a threatened minority in the very city that they built. Others regret that the community never assimilated, missing out on having a place at the table in postcolonial India.

Chaiwala could never have foreseen this future. His strong pride in the Parsis' distinct identity and destiny as a select elite is evident in his writing. Insofar as his novel's narrative was anchored in the desire to staunchly defend the Parsis' cultural heritage and Zoroastrian religion, he would not be an unusual figure in the city today.

I gained an understanding of Chaiwala's cultural world from my conversations, but I still had to find the missing text. Every time I was in Mumbai for research, I continued my hunt. The breakthrough came at the end of 2003, nearly three years after I had first found the novel in London.

In my search for Chaiwala's novel in Mumbai's libraries, I had neglected the Secretariat Library, which is housed in the same building as the Asiatic Society. Walking through it on the way to the Asiatic Society, I had scarcely given a second glance to its reading room crowded with government servants and students reading newspapers and popular magazines. When I drew a blank in the Asiatic Society's vaunted collection, I resumed my search in other libraries. With those yielding nothing, I wondered if Chaiwala had sent his novel only to London. Even if he had deigned to send it to the city's libraries, the typescript might have been subject to the mercies of the notoriously cavalier Indian librarians.

It was then that I remembered the row of dusty card catalogues in the Secretariat's reading room. Without much hope, I decided to try my luck. It was the day before I was to leave Mumbai and there was little else to do. Billowing dust rose when I forced open the rickety drawers of the jammed card catalogue, searching the entries on authors. Imagine my amazement when I found not one, but two entries for P.J. Chevalier! The first was for *Sixty-Seven Poems*, the second for *Tower of Silence*. I filled out two slips immediately, requisitioning both. Heart pounding and fingers nervously drumming on the desk, I waited. Thirty minutes later, the library peon walked into the reading room and summoned me to the librarian's desk. He handed me a bound volume of 'Sixty-Seven Poems'. The other book, he informed me, was untraceable. Then he left.

Crestfallen, I returned to my desk and desultorily read Chaiwala's poems. 'Amy' was a long poem about the poet's passion for another man's wife. Yet another, 'The Same Old Cry' railed against the conventional morality that forbade this love. Yet another was a diatribe against usurers of all faiths. The passion was palpable but the quality was uniformly mediocre. I had hit a low point, the dejection of not finding *Tower of Silence* compounded by reading Chaiwala's depressing poetry. Nonetheless, I decided to make one more try.

I walked up to the librarian and struck up a

conversation about the library. She asked me about my research and my teaching position at Princeton University. She told me about herself and her visit to Cleveland where her son worked. I told her about finding Chaiwala's incomplete novel at the British Library and my fruitless search for copies in Mumbai's libraries. It was quite possible, I told her, that her library was the only one with the complete typescript of an important novel. As I spoke, the peon who had been listening to our conversation, the same one who had told me that *Tower of Silence* was untraceable, perked up. He asked me to write down the name once again on a slip of paper. Five minutes later, he returned with a bound copy of the complete novel. I had not been wrong about the Secretariat Library possibly being the only one in the world with a complete typescript. There was joy all around.

THE TEXT

At the center of *Tower of Silence* is an actual incident. In 1923, *The Graphic*, a London weekly, published an article on the Tower of Silence, or *dokhma*, in PunePune.1 It described, without negative judgment, the Parsi practice of leaving their dead in the tower's well to be devoured by vultures. Accompanying the article were two illustrations. One was a photograph of the *dokhma*, a circular stone structure rising about 25 feet in height, with a flock of vultures sitting on top. The centrepiece, however, was a large aerial photograph of the Parsi dead in the well of the Tower.

The photograph created a stir in Mumbai. Sir Jamsetji Jejeebhoy, the chairman of the Parsi Punchayet, conveyed the outrage of the community to the Governor of Bombay, Lord George Lloyd. The Governor sent a telegram to the Secretary of State for India in London, communicating the sense of indignation among the Parsis and requesting that the magazine's editor be persuaded to destroy the photographic plate and the negative.[2] The Secretary of State promptly wrote to *The Graphic*'s editor, who promised to destroy the plate and to ask the photographer to destroy the negative. The editor assured the Secretary of State that the photographer, although a European, was not an official, enabling the colonial government to plead non-complicity in the offending act. He also apologized for having violated Parsi religious sentiments, though of course that was not the intention. Like any editor, he was simply struck by the photograph's novelty.

In fact, the West was morbidly fascinated with the Parsi practice of disposing of their dead. In 1912, a British soldier was accused of entering the Tower of Silence in Pune, whereupon he was seized and bound by several men.[3] The *Times of India* published a review of a Mills and Boon book of short stories by Maude Annesley titled *Nights and Days*.[4] Among the stories was one called 'The Tower of Silence', detailing the experiences of an English lady married to an Oxford-educated Parsi millionaire in Bombay. Apparently, the story ended with the lady's suicidal and melodramatic entry into the well of a Tower of Silence where a Parsi priest pointed a chilling and calamitous finger to her doom. The reviewer ended by advising the Bombay Police to read the story to learn unknown details about Parsi customs.

More literary help awaited the Bombay Police. In 1920, the *Boston Globe* published a detective story by R.T.M. Scott, 'Smith of the C.I.D.: The Towers of Silence.'[5] The story was about a US senator who has gone missing in Bombay. Smith, a Bombay Police detective, cracks the mystery as he, along with his Indian helpers, the senator's secretary and the American counsel climb under the cover of darkness into the Tower of Silence on Malabar Hill. They find the senator in the well of the tower into which he had been lured and abandoned to the vultures by his scheming secretary. The secretary meets his just desserts by being abandoned to a similar fate. To great Parsi outrage, his flesh-stripped skeleton is discovered in the well a few days later.

Meanwhile, aircraft were reported flying over dokhmas in spite of the indignation of the Parsis. A Texan reported in 1920 that a British pilot might have finally revealed the long-cherished secrets of the Towers by flying over them.[6] The newspaper noted that the aviator's flight had provoked furious protests, but it went on to feed the readers' ghoulish appetite for details about vultures lying in wait for the dead bodies. Not to be outdone, the *New York Times* published a long story on the Parsis; it described their history, religion and prominent place in business, but the main focus was on the Tower of Silence.[7]

Chaiwala's novel was composed in the context of

this perverse obsession with Parsi mortuary practices, the most egregious example of it being the publication of the aerial photograph in *The Graphic*. But while others clamoured for legal action against the magazine, the editor and the photographer, Chaiwala exacted retribution in fiction.

FINDING CHAIWALA

What was in his biography that explained his literary ambition? Who was this Parsi with the nom de plume of Chevalier?

I now had the complete novel but had made little progress in finding details about Chaiwala. Further consultation of *Thacker's India Directory* and *Times of India Directory and Calendar* revealed that his address had changed in 1931 from Tardeo to Dadar. He was listed as a resident of Imperial Mahal, Vincent Road (presently, Ambedkar Road on Khodadad Circle). This entry was repeated for the next two years, after which his name disappears from the directories. A visit to the building proved fruitless. No one had heard of Chaiwala, let alone remembered him. He did not appear in Pune directories either, casting doubt on my speculation that he had moved back there.

The next stop was the Parsi Punchayet, the apex administrative body of the Parsi community. I was received cordially at the Punchayet's office on Dadabhai Naoroji Road, but the officials threw up their hands when I asked to see their death records. 'If you don't know when he died, then it is like looking for a needle in a haystack!' I was referred to another official who was reputed to know all about the days of yore. I walked over to the desk of a genial looking elderly gentleman. When I explained my purpose, he sighed and said: 'That's like looking for a needle in a haystack'. Over the next hour or so, he treated me to a barrage of aphorisms as he swiftly moved away from my inquiry to the subject of the state of the Parsis and the city. The substance of what he said was familiar. By now I had heard several variations of his discourse on the unique history of the Parsis, how their heyday coincided with the best times of the city, and how their marginalization was followed by Mumbai's decline and disarray. But the aphorisms that punctuated his speech and his archaic, Victorian English immediately reminded me of Chaiwala's novel. The visit, after all, had not been pointless. I had caught a glimpse of my author and his milieu in this Punchayet official's language.

In 2003, I placed an advertisement in *Parsiana*, the Parsi journal circulated worldwide, requesting information on Chaiwala. I received no helpful response. In 2013, I published another advertisement in *Jam-e-Jamshed*. But again, no response was forthcoming.

Meanwhile, I was beginning to build Chaiwala's portrait. A search in the *Bombay University Calendar* revealed that he matriculated from Tutorial High School, Bombay, in 1914. This was my cue to visit the school, now called Master Tutorial High School. Located near Kennedy Bridge, the school is housed in an old building that has seen better days. The principal, Peter D'Costa, was seated behind a desk in a small room, surrounded by a clutter of files and deep into office work with his associate. My presence was obviously inconvenient, but he very kindly and promptly requisitioned a thick, bound volume called the General Register. I carefully turned its yellowed, crumbling pages, running my finger over each numbered entry. My heart stopped when I spotted the entry – Peroshaw Jamshedji Chaewala. The register recorded that he was admitted to the school on 14 January 1913, and that his previous school was the Pune Native Institution. I also discovered that his younger brother Behram, born in 1898 and previously at St. Vincent's in Pune, was admitted at the same time. So were his sisters – Falak, born in 1902, previously at Sir C J Readymoney Girl's School, Pune, and the 1906-born Shirin. Evidently, the family had moved from Pune to Bombay, where the children were enrolled at the same co-educational school that, Mr D'Costa explained, was preponderantly Parsi at that time.

Having matriculated from high school, Mr Chaiwala joined Wilson College. According to the *Bombay University Calendar*, he passed the first year certificate examination in 1916 and Intermediate in Arts in 1917, studying Logic and French (perhaps explaining his adoption of the moniker Chevalier). He earned a BA in Philosophy in 1922. A visit to Wilson College proved rewarding. I was lucky once again to run into a very cooperative and forthcoming Vice-Principal, Professor Shehernaz Nalwalla. A Parsi herself, she got caught up in my enthusiasm, requisitioning old college registers and calling acquaintances for information. The records indicated that Chaiwala, or Chaewala, as his name was spelt in the register, was active in the college literary society, giving lectures on such diverse subjects as 'English humourists of the 18th century', 'The Gods of India' and 'Love.'8 He did not win any prizes or scholarships, and never passed his examinations in the first or second divisions but always in the lowest category – the pass class.

However, lack of academic excellence did not imply an absence of intellectual ambition. He was reported to have opened a debate on 'It is the Man that makes the Woman' organized by the Zoroastrian Brotherhood in October 1918.[9] A decade later, when he was already PJ Chevalier, he wrote a Gujarati play, 'Pussyfoot' (Char Angelio in Gujarati, meaning four-toed ones), which was staged by the Empire Poetry League at Excelsior Theatre.[10] Miss Falakbanu Jamsetjee Chaiwala, a student of Elphinstone College, and the secretary of the Empire Poetry League, had initiated this event to support the Sir Leslie Wilson Hospital Fund. Her brother, the playwright PJ Chevalier, was the Vice-President of the League. Including both male and female actors in defiance of tradition, the 'serio-comic' play, as it was described, was about two brokers who set out to loot people in a scientific manner while forming a pact to test each other's wives.

PJ Chevalier was not done yet. Having already written a novel and staged his play, he threw his hat in the ring for the 1929 elections to the Bombay Municipal Council.

Addressing a 'sparsely attended gathering of voters' at Sir Cowasji Jehangir Hall organized by Ratheshtar Mandal, a Parsi organization for the 'moral upliftment' of the community, he asked that a chance be given to 'young blood'. He promised to work for better relations between communities, promote education and improve the conditions of poor municipal employees.11 This is where things get mysterious again. The *Times of India* lists him as one of the candidates in the D ward (Girgaum), but his name does not appear in the list of winners and losers.12 Perhaps he failed to actually file his election papers even as he campaigned as a candidate. Whatever the case, he had managed, once again, to throw mystery over himself.

But as I read and re-read the now complete text of *Tower of Silence*, the mystery began to clear. I began to understand that he was both Chaiwala and Chevalier. Like many Parsis I had encountered during my search, he took deep pride in his Parsi identity. This is evident in *Tower of Silence*. The text offers a primer on Parsi manners, customs, and clothing – all related to purity rituals that Zoroastrians had practiced for millennia. These practices, he wrote, were not based on blind faith but scientific facts, now proven by Western science. This was a common belief among the intelligentsia in the colonies. Hindu intellectuals also, for instance, claimed that modern Western science affirmed the scientific validity of the principles and practices advocated by the ancient Vedas. Beram, the Parsi protagonist possibly named after Chaiwala's younger brother, embodies the cultural qualities widely claimed by indigenous intellectuals in the colonies.

But Beram is not just another indigenous figure. As a Parsi, he is special. Chaiwala is angered by the ignorance of Englishmen who mistake a Parsi for just another Indian. Beram is from the East, but his person combines the vast and time-tested ancient wisdom of the Parsis with the modern scientific and technological arts of the West. He is a Chaiwala who can also pass off as a Chevalier.

Although Beram's adversaries in the novel are British, he is not a nationalist. He duels with the British to avenge Parsi honour, but it is an engagement of equals, not between the colonizer and the colonized. Chaiwala wrote at a time when Gandhian mass nationalism was already in full flow, including in his native Bombay, but there is scant reflection of anti-colonial politics in the novel. Indeed, the text frequently expresses an admiration for British customs and manners.

Chaiwala treats the Western landscape as if it were his own. His characters navigate the London streets and go in and out of hotels and inns with ease. He uses the details of the 1923 Lympne air show to great narrative effect. His choice of Sexton Blake, the popular fictional detective, as Beram's adversary reveals his knowledge of the popular English cultural milieu of the period. As Beram plays a cat-and-mouse game with Sexton Blake and his assistant Tinker, the action does not appear as a clash of cultures but as a contest of wits between individuals who share a vocabulary but pursue different goals. He uses English details with authority, as if he grew up with them. The novel even shares the contemporary British attitude towards the Nagas, regarding them as savages.

The prose style wavers between the Victorian language of Charles Dickens and the more fast-paced popular style of Edgar Rice Burroughs and other fiction writers of the period. The characters speak in the diction appropriate to their class and station in life. At times there are long sentences, strung out with semicolons, in hyperbolic language. But the tale itself is very much like the fiction of Edgar Rice Burroughs, with travels to exotic lands and a transcontinental chase. Poisons, magical drugs and a fight unto death between a cobra and a mongoose amplify the suspense and adventure. Secret cellars and disguises add mystery and provide twists to the narrative.

Even as occult powers and sorcery punctuate the story, the setting is thoroughly modern. Industrial modernity in the form of planes, trains and automobiles figure prominently. Chaiwala shows off his knowledge of firearms and explosives, investigative techniques and deductive reasoning as his characters race around London in expensive Rolls Royce and Mercedes automobiles.

Modern imperial geography also underpins the novel as the story moves between Britain, India and Burma. Easing the movement of the narrative across imperial territories is a cultural circuit, a cosmopolitan milieu that Chaiwala regards as wholly natural. Beram dwells in this milieu while proudly wearing his Parsi identity.

In this sense, the novel bears the mark of its time, expressing the fable of Bombay as a cosmopolitan city. Even as the narrative action brings the city, high and low, into view, what makes it a Bombay novel is its imaginative texture. *Tower of Silence* shows an intimate knowledge of Bombay as the story unfolds in places like the Taj Mahal Hotel, bars, the Parsi colonies, Colaba, Nepean Sea Road, Crawford Market and the Esplanade police station. But underlying it is the city's mythic image. A Bombay man, Chaiwala affirms this image as he calls the city 'gay and cosmopolitan', a heady mix of polyglot culture and fast life. It is this urban sensibility of Bombay that underwrites the novel. Even when the action takes place elsewhere, what guides it is a cosmopolitan worldview characteristic of the colonial city. To be sure, this cosmopolitanism was blind to its imperial and class underpinnings. But as a product of this world, Beram comfortably inhabits its cultural milieu so long as his Parsi identity and heritage are not threatened.

I had not found all of Chaiwala's biographical details. A second visit to the Parsi Punchayet, eased by weighty recommendations, did not yield fresh information. I was given access to the death registers, but unfortunately, only those dating from 1961 have been preserved. In any case, neither Chaiwala nor Chevalier showed up in the records. 'He could have died in 1933 or migrated', a friendly Punchayet official told me. 'Not to be a wet blanket, but without more details, it is like…' he hesitated for a moment as he searched for the right words. '...It is like – what do they say – looking for a needle in a haystack!' There was that phrase again, but it no longer amused me. Seeing my dejected face, he tried to cheer me up. 'It is for a novel, right? This makes for an even better story! Chaiwala disappears into thin air!' He was right. Like the characters in his novel, Chaiwala had done a masterful disappearing act. He was gone. Without a trace.

But I had found him: in the *Tower of Silence* and the Parsi discourse in Bombay. From the pages of the text, he emerged as someone completely at home in the Anglophone cultural world so long as it did not imperil his identity as a Parsi. . He was obviously well-travelled and well-read. One of his characters could shoot with 'the eye of Locksley' (Robin Hood) and could tell you how to journey from Rangoon to Putao. Chaiwala had disarming ambition and drive. Though he had no poetic talents, he self-published both a collection of his verse and a rollicking detective novel. He was very cosmopolitan. And, of course, very Bombay.

NOTES

1   *The Graphic*, 108:2804 (25 August 1923)

2   British Library, Oriental and India Office Collection: IOR/L/P&J/6/1862, File 5203. The controversy in Bombay over this incident is described in Mitra Sharafi's, *Law and Identity in Colonial South Asia: Parsi Legal Culture, 1772-1947*. (Forthcoming Cambridge: Cambridge University Press, 2014}

3   'Assault on a Soldier: Towers of Silence Incident', *Times of India*, 10 June 1913.

4   'Recent Fiction', *Times of India*, 30 October 2012.

5   *Boston Globe*, 11 March 1923.

6   'Exotic Things Stir Indians', *Los Angeles Times*, 6 June 1920.

7   'Sun Worshippers: A Power in India', *New York Times*, 16 March 1924.

8   *The Wilsonian* (Pune: The Scottish Mission Industries Company Limited), for the years 1916, 1917 and 1918.

9   'Bombay Engagements', *Times of India*, 5 October 1918.

10 'Parsi Theatricals', *Times of India*, 19 November 1928.

11 'Bombay Municipal Elections: Appeal to Voters', *Times of India*, 14 January 1929.

12 'Bombay Municipal Elections: Keen Canvassing', *Times of India*, 29 January 1929; and 'Strength of Progressives and Nationalists', *Times of India*, 31 January 1929.

CHAPTER I

India is a great peninsula located in the south of Asia. The whole of its western coast is called Bombay Presidency where Bombay is the chief town and principal seaport. Poona, about four hour's journey from Bombay by the Great Indian Peninsula Railway, is a military station of no mean importance. It is also the summer seat of the government, when the heat in Bombay is more than conveniently bearable. The Poona racecourse, under the control of the Western Indian Turf Club, is the envy of the whole of Bombay Presidency.

The town is divided into two sections. The most densely populated area is called the 'City', while the extensive area of neat streets with pleasant little bungalows on either side, surrounded by well-cared for gardens, is termed the 'Camp'. It is in the Camp that the well-to-do live, particularly those who have resigned from daily activities, either after a long meritorious government service or from their own businesses.

To the north of the Camp, except for a few bungalows with vast grounds, the whole of the surrounding country is an open plain, unkempt but picturesque, stretching for miles around. It is also where the solitary structure of the Tower of Silence stands, on one of the highest hills that rings the town on three sides.

At 2 p.m. one cloudless day in April, the hottest month of the year, through the heat waves that one could clearly see and feel, a tiny speck appeared in the sky moving from the racecourse side in the direction of the Tower of Silence.

At first, it could perhaps be taken for a solitary eagle basking in the penetrating rays of the sun. But on second thoughts, a keen observer would not fail to note that this species usually goes up in groups and that an eagle would scarcely fly as a crow does in a straight line, but in gentle curves, floating up and down and forward as eagles alone can do. Nor could it be a crow, for that black gentleman could never dream of reaching such an immense height. The next explanation was simple, but it seemed impossible for a full-sized aeroplane to be seen in this part of India. As the speck drew nearer and nearer, it seemed to grow larger at every moment, till it was overhead at an angle of forty-five degrees. It was so high that its presence would never have been detected unless someone had noticed it flying above. Over the next few minutes, it flew once overhead and then moved away into the void. Gleaming white in the glaring light and the almost unbearable heat of the sun, it went in the opposite direction from whence it came, growing smaller and smaller as it flew away from the Tower of Silence.

The speck then disappeared over the horizon. If an observer had by some chance seen the aeroplane's approach during the terrible heat of the noonday sun, he would soon have lost interest. Whether it was a dodge, or it had reached the point from which it was to double back to its goal, subsequent events were to prove. But return it did.

Once again, it approached at an angle of about forty-five degrees, but this time it seemed to fly closer to the ground. For the first time, the outlines of the machine were visible. It appeared to be a powerfully built light craft, with engines that were quiet, yet sure, strong and smoothly rhythmical. It hovered for a few moments, until it attained an angle of sixty to seventy degrees.

All of a sudden, it swooped down recklessly in a neat dive towards the ground. It continued its crazy course till it seemed that it would, without the least doubt, crash to the ground and lie there in a mangled, burning heap. It was as if the man in control had lost his nerve. But its mad career was suddenly checked. Then, as it appeared to right itself, the plane began to play somersaults like a big fluttering kite shot in one wing that is struggling to stay in the air to stop itself from falling in a plumb line to the ground.

Just when the case seemed hopeless, the plane stopped its fatal descent with a loud roar and began to move forward in large circles, now flying upside down. If the airman and the solitary passenger had not been securely strapped onto their seats, they would without a doubt have dropped onto the hard ground beneath and been transformed in a trice into an unnerving mass of shapeless pulp. The semi-unruffled 'phuts! phuts!' of the engine created no stir in the neighbourhood, for it appeared like the familiar sound of the military having their target practice beyond the neighbouring hills. If the noise seemed at all out of the ordinary, it was perhaps explained away as something more than usual having transpired at the shooting range.

The plane had now righted itself but nevertheless flew aimlessly in a zig-zag path, the airman shaping its course in huge downward curves. It was indeed most curious! Was there some unforeseen magnetic influence that was holding the plane about the place?

Whether it would dive or volplane or move around in huge meaningless circles, it seemed unable to tear itself away from the sombre grey-white presence of the Tower of Silence. Was it the idle curiosity of an unbeliever to gaze upon the scene and profane the place or was there some other deliberate mathematical calculation with a grim purpose behind it?

Once more, the machine tilted dangerously to one side, but to one who understood aircraft, it appeared more of a device than an outcome of accident. It was again on the point of turning upside down when it righted itself in the nick of time. At that precise moment, a bright star-like object fell with a heavy dull speed in a straight line into the structure of the Tower of Silence and disappeared into its deep and awesome depth.

But for the intense light of the pitiless sun, the bright object that fell from the plane would have appeared as fleeting as a rocket, lost to sight in a few moments once it dropped into the hollow space underneath. Immediately the object penetrated the dark well-like interior of the grim structure, a brightness never seen there before brought into glaring relief the nerve-wracking objects reposing in its bosom.

One whole mound of skeletons, in all manner of poses, lay in a mouldering heap. The arms and legs of some were entwined around their own frames or that of their neighbours. Along the border of the twenty-foot thick wall of the well too, could be seen some half-a-dozen skeletons in different postures. One was lying flat on its back with its face upturned, the eyeless sockets gazing defiantly up in silent mockery at the blazing sun's burning rays. Another lay face down as if in utter sorrow and lamentation for forsaking the alluring rich world at so unseemly a moment.

Of the couple of freshly brought in bodies, one was turned sideways in a pose of peace and quietude. Its upper portion was quite devoid of flesh while the side in contact with the marble stones beneath was intact. So it was with the other corpse but for one difference. Whereas the former was allowed to maintain its pose of sleep, the latter was being turned over by some three or four huge dark forms, working in unison. The side facing the sun almost immediately suffered from the ruthless, cruel beaks of the vultures. For a brief moment, they crouched down in a highly tense and aggravated attitude at being thus unceremoniously disturbed by the object that fell in a sparkling glare into the dark abyss-like pit.

It was very queer, but no sooner had the gruesome

objects in the well of the Tower of Silence come out in clear relief, than the aeroplane recovered from its dangerous plight. It quivered a little, stood still for one long moment and then rose up in a graceful curve, as if sighing in relief for avoiding meeting a revolting death in the pit beneath.

In that brief moment as the clock struck 2 p.m., as the plane appeared to be stock-still, there was a sharp, low, metallic, shutter-like click. A trained ear could scarcely have failed to explain the brazen drama enacted in that tragic moment.

'Click'. So the chapter ended, bringing in its trail intense mental suffering to many and heralding several breath-stealing events that were to follow in quick succession.

Chapter II

Sirdar Kaidokad Aspandad, head priest of the Deccan, was taking his afternoon nap. He was peacefully sleeping on his bed in a beautifully furnished room of an imposing bungalow that was his ancestral property. The adjoining historical building was chiefly used for keeping the sacred fire, whose rightful guardian he was. This was the Atasberam, the father of all the temples in the Deccan.

One could reasonably think that the virtue of one fire is the same as any other. It gives the same majestic glow with which no one can take liberty with impunity. It appears to have the same one quality of inner pervading virtue, whether in a solitary log of wood or in a molten furnace. On the surface, this may all appear very true. But it must not be forgotten that the civilization of Persia and the ascendancy of the Parsees in Irania, the faithful followers of the Prophet Zoroaster, dates from 5000 BC. So Zoroastrianism has flourished for nearly 7000 years, and it is the flame from the sacred ball of fire handed down to his followers by Zoroaster that is still preserved in a secret place in India. The betrayal of this place would be a death sentence for us, an automatic opening of the golden gate into the kingdom of heaven.

To the ordinary layman, it might appear as a truism that the inner virtue of a glowing coal is the same as that of any other burning ember. But there is a fundamental difference according to Zoroastrian philosophy. It rightly teaches its followers that even as the degree of fire varies according to the fuel supplied to it, or to be exact, an intermixture of air and fuel, so does its virtue differ comparatively.

For instance, the fire originating from an impure heap of faggots, leaves and other rubbish saturated in kerosene oil is undoubtedly inferior in quality and health-giving benefits to one emanating from a heap of sandalwood chips burnt in a pure atmosphere on a block of marble and accompanied by the determined chantings of reverent priests, trained over thousands of years in the art of evoking a flame second only in virtue to the life-giving glow of the sun. It cannot be denied that the Zoroastrians are past masters in this art of purifying and enhancing the virtue of fire. Their chants and the powerful electrically magnetic vibrating effects that their voices produce in unison are strong enough to literally snap the fetters of the most finely tempered steel. Even an ordinary semi-serious priest or zealous layman can break a glass tumbler to splinters by no other outward agency than the force of the magical vibrations of his sweet chants.

The fire temple in the keeping of Sirdar Kaidokad Aspandad contains the purest of pure fire, burning in a huge silver receptacle and ignited directly from the original ball of fire handed down by Zoroaster. Its sacredness to the Zoroastrians can be seen from the intrinsic benefits that it confers on those who pray before it with faith. Hence the epithet fire worshippers, though in reality there is no actual fire worshipping but only the sober acknowledgement of the majestic glow of the fire as the best emblem of the creator, the one and only omnipotent god, the source of purity and righteousness, the beginning and end of the universe.

The keeper of the flame, the head priest of Atasberam, was sixty years old. In spite of his age, he seemed to be in excellent health due to a religiously led life. He took up the complete length of the bed, for he was not of insignificant stature. He was also of ample proportions with bones covered by a shapely white mass of flesh and muscles. He had well-cropped hair and his face was covered with a huge but carefully combed silvery-gray beard. His face had a benevolent expression with the exception of the eyes that seemed to contain something deep and unfathomable.

As a rule, he did not suffer from the disturbing dreams that trouble others in their sleep. His sleep was almost childlike and peaceful. But on this particular afternoon, when the hidden shutter three miles away registered that fatal 'Click', his peaceful slumber was most dreadfully disturbed. On that sultry afternoon of the unbearable Indian summer, when men, beasts and birds seemed glad to escape from its tormenting influence, there was that sound.

'Click'.

At that very moment, the whole atmosphere around the sleeping head priest became disturbed. The 'click' let loose, as it were, some hidden magnetic button, sending in all directions some hidden and mysterious influences miles away, greatly disturbing the mental plane of interested and advanced personages like the old priest.

All of a sudden, he was conscious of a sudden burden settling on the seat of his peaceful soul. It was no dream or cruel trick of the mind. It was a sort of message, a mute realization, the passing of spirit into spirit, mysterious and inexplicable. It was not an ordinary telepathic message. There was no agent at the other extremity sending the message. Rather, it was the finely developed something in the man that made him instantly aware of impending danger, the realization of the information not vouchsafed by any sentient being.

A secret was out. Some foreign eyes had defiled the tranquil atmosphere either of a place of worship there in Poona or elsewhere. It was a vague premonition and realization that he was wanting in the task he had been set to safeguard by heaven. The magnetic well had been disturbed by a foreign and invisible element entering into it, its unwarrantable impure immersion causing ripples large and small.

He lay on his back in an almost cataleptic condition. Though his eyes were shut, his sense of hearing grew intensely acute. His mind, or his very soul as it were, appeared to come out of his body, hovering in close proximity to it, or around the temple he was guarding, or miles away where some zealously guarded secret shrines reposed in complete security.

Lying thus in a tense attitude of grim expectation, outwardly calm yet inwardly raging, he failed to gauge the cause of his agitation. Nevertheless he felt certain that others who were as inwardly powerful as himself must also have received this message of inexplicable foreboding. So he tried to enter into mental communication with the guardians of four other smaller temples situated in the town. But news that he could easily have received during normal times through his great powers accumulated over half a century failed him at that moment, and his soul grieved at the prospect of losing these powers in so unaccountable a manner.

Something was terribly wrong somewhere and he could not put his finger on the spot. What could it be?

CHAPTER III

At the Batliwala Agiary, one of the four smaller temples, a ceremony of unique importance was being performed.

Faresta, invoking the thirty-three ministers (angels) of god, lacks even the slightest personal factor, as it is a thanksgiving for benefits already received rather than a request for fresh favours from god. On such occasions an offering is made of sweet-scented flowers of the most delicate Indian perfume, such as red and creamy white roses, lilywhite chambalis and fragrant mogras. A variety of the most delicious fruits are also offered in pretty silver dishes and utensils, along with the most agreeable and highly palatable sweet dishes.

There is of course a constant burning of costly incense and pure chips of sandalwood, agar, loban, etc. on glowing coals in a beautifully designed small silver receptacle. Eight priests, all dressed in white with snow-white pieces of rich muslin tied about their noses and hanging before their lips, were deeply engrossed in the rhythmical songs of Zoroaster in praise of God and his ministering angels that were the most authentic and brought the most positive results.

Then, at 2 p.m. there was that sound.

'Click'

The atmosphere in the temple, surcharged as it was by the holy vibrations, raged into unimagined violence. For a second or two, the jaws of the officiating priests remained gaping wide open. Their voices seemed to die away at the very threshold of their throats. A horrified look crept into their eyes as if they suffered from a sudden shock of high electric voltage. Unconscious of their surroundings, the people sitting around them were ignorant of what was passing through their minds.

It was as if an aperture in their vision shot open and they just managed to catch sight of sad receding forms of the heavenly invoked beings before they vanished into obscurity. They were aware that it was no mere illusion. They knew that what was taking place was certainly not the product of imagination but a matter of fact. To all outward appearances the eight priests appeared calm but a silent mental message passed through their minds and each one of them knew for certain that all the other seven had experienced what he had but a moment ago. In unison, their thoughts were that something was terribly wrong.

ᵕ᷾ ᪥

At around 1 p.m., in a middle class quarter of a street in Poona, long rows of chairs were placed on the side facing a line of a half-a-dozen neighbouring houses. On the verandah of the centre house, a huge copper vessel filled with well water stood on an iron stand, with a small German silver lota, or cup, placed beside it.

People dressed in white, with long coats and their national head gear, either a pheta or pagree, arrived one by one. Also seen arriving in batches of two, or three or four, were ladies young and old, dressed in sable-black sarees with sapat on their feet. The men settled themselves on the rows of chairs, after washing their faces with the water from the copper utensil prior to performing a short thread prayer. The womenfolk proceeded straight away into the inner room. Immediately on entry, each woman would stoop low before the cold body and bow to it. After making a reverential obeisance, they took their seats, squatting cross-legged on the ground that was covered with white sheets.

They sat in a semi curve, in the hollow of which was a figure wrapped in white muslin. A silver utensil containing glowing coals and burning incense lay between the corpse and the two officiating priests who were mumbling prayers in a slow rhythmical intonation. The prone figure was lying on slabs of stone carved especially for the grim purpose. Its legs were crossed as were its arms. Securely wrapped from the neck downward in white muslin, only the face was visible.

And what a face it was. Alabaster white, the lips slightly parted, revealing an exquisite double row of pearly white teeth with an inexplicable smile, seeming joyous at leaving behind the heavy cares and worries of this world. The serene smile indicated the heavenly bliss in crossing over the very threshold of paradise with but a slight tinge of sadness for having left behind him his dear ones. The forehead was high without a single wrinkle upon it. One or two stray locks of hair that peeped out gave an indication of the wealth of gold on the scalp while the nose was the delicate replica of a Grecian pattern.

The hall was now full of women; there were rich and poor, young and old, pensive and thoughtless, mothers and daughters, all of them on one common platform performing their bounden homage to the grim penalty that sooner or later they would all have to pay when life's reel of golden thread either fairly spun out or snapped in twain at an untimely moment.

When more priests arrived, the final ceremony began, prior to the body being taken to the Tower of Silence a mile or two away. The room was full of the pleasant smell of rich sandalwood burning. The mood was sombre as befitted the occasion. The mother, wife and the three very beautiful young daughters of the dead man were lamenting their insufferable loss. The heartbreaking sobs of the mother and wife and other close relatives, and the loud lamentations of the three innocent girls, brought forth an abundance of sympathetic tears from the whole congregation. The only son of the dead man, standing on the threshold of the doorway from where the body of his beloved father would be taken away, was crying his heart out in silent suppressed sobs.

The clock, hanging high on the wall appeared no less sombre. An observer would have noticed the due significance of the larger hand approaching its zenith, while the smaller hand pointed at the figure two.

'Click'.

Two miles away from the origin of the terrible sound, the chanting of the five priests, two near the doorstep, two near the body and one keeping alive the flame with rich incense, died away. A lightning intercommunicative shock passed through their minds. Something had happened.

As the hour for parting drew neigh, the wife was frantic with grief. The mother looked with devotion at her dead son's face, quite oblivious of the world around her, when, horror of horrors, she gave out one loud piercing shriek. Pointing her right-hand finger towards the face of her dead son, she stared at it with horror-stricken eyes mixed with unbelieving unadulterated joy for a moment and then fell face forward in a dead faint.

Her scream attracted the attention of others who turned their eyes towards the point she had indicated. What they saw sent shivers down their spines, though it was a sight that ought to have made them happy.

Gradually, very gradually, almost with measured methodical precision, the smiling parting lips of the stone-cold form closed over the shining rows of pearl-white teeth. The air of sublimity imperceptibly disappeared, and was replaced by a mournful frown.

Something was terribly wrong somewhere. What could it be?

❧ ❦

Another scene played out in a vault of huge proportions in an excellently preserved place in a certain town, the most secretive place of fire worship in India. The exact location of the place would serve us no good purpose here.

It was here that the fire, handed down to his followers by Zoroaster and that has been constantly kept burning, was seen in all its glory, glowing on a unique receptacle of precious elements. A very important ceremony was taking place before the *Kabla*, the sacred fire. It was Nowjot, the thread ceremony. A child of nine years was being inducted into the religion of his forefathers. The priests were just nearing the end of their sacred recital of the lengthy ceremony when, miles away, there was that sound.

'Click'.

The officiating priests and the boy undergoing the ceremony got shocks through their very beings as if some unseen force had knocked against them. One of the priests, whose exclusive duty was to continually feed the fire, was in the act of putting a fragrant piece of agar on the sacred flame when innumerable meteor-like sparks burst from the fire and spread all around, almost enveloping him. A veritable shower of bright sparks, all vivified and most beautiful in their burning anger, flew past the priests and right through the door, before the eyes of the congregation. But outside, the atmosphere was dead calm, without a vestige of wind. Not a leaf stirred.

Every priest gathered there knew that a vital spark had escaped the secret fire. Outwardly they managed to remain calm and sober. It was only after the guests had departed that they could meditate upon the occurrence. They came to the same conclusion as any other reasonable person would. Something was terribly wrong.

CHAPTER IV

The offices of *The Graphic* monthly were situated in an imposing building. The traffic was flowing as usual when a big touring Rolls Royce was seen wading through the throng of passersby.

On the richly upholstered rear seat, a slim young man sat with a smile hovering on his lips, the upper part of which was adorned with a golden-brown moustache. He had a platinum framed monocle in his left eye from which dangled a golden chain. The other end of the chain was attached to a vest button by a beautiful white diamond pin that sparkled brilliantly in the sunlight.

The young man was wearing an exquisitely tailored navy-blue serge lounge suit. He wore a matching tie, and jet-black rubber-heeled glace kid boots. His hair was neatly combed and nicely groomed. His hat was lying on the seat beside him. It was not easy to guess his nationality, except to know from his aspect and general bearing that he appeared to be an ordinary European, although his skin was tanned like that of a man used to extensive travel in sultry climes. He had a fine cast of features and a shapely Roman nose. His lips were of ordinary size, neither thin nor large, but red with pure blood. His cheeks had a slight inclination for hollow. His high and shapely forehead did not fail to signify the extraordinary intelligence lurking in the brain stored behind.

The young man's face was most expressive and his inner thoughts seemed clearly mirrored to the gaze of any casual observer. It gave him that frank aspect which helped the possessor much in business. He never took pains to hide his everyday thoughts but could do so when the occasion demanded it.

He did suffer from a couple of peculiarities but only a keen analyst of human nature would be able to discern them. In fact, it would require an expert analytical psychologist to read the signs. Whenever he was irritated or grappling with the solution of a problem, his left eye would contract ever so slightly. This slight contraction was the only sign of his powerful brain's lightning-like deductions and the extraordinary intelligence residing in those silent orbs.

The second peculiarity was a bit more out of the ordinary. A tremor would pass through the fingertips of his right hand at critical moments. If minutely observed, if he held a cup of tea or a tumbler of iced water for instance, the utensil would distinctly be seen to shake. While some experts might be led to believe it to be a sign of palsy striking at an early age, others might conclude that such a state was a consequence of weakness of the body and shattered nerves. At times, the powerful mental thought currents would find egress with such force and concentrated power that his fingertips actually vibrated with the passing energy like the wires of a sensitive electric machine.

As a matter of fact, the occupant of the car was in full bloom and vigour of health. When he willed it, his fingers would grow firm as a rock and take a grip on a person or thing which could not be easily shifted with any degree of comfort. When irritated or in deep thought, he was at times entirely unaware that these signs betrayed his true feelings. However, they would last only for a few moments and then vanish.

The young man was also a true and a rare votary of the occult science, a past master in the mystical science of hypnotism. In him, the knowledge of the shrewd east was liberally blended with that of the west. He pursued the Western mode of conveying thought, but the real scientific little-known maxims that he applied savoured that of the East; he brought together the substance of the East and the mode of the West.

His unique self-training made his thoughts and his willpower so extraordinarily keen and powerful that, mere thoughts though they may be, they were as solid as lead and if sent in somebody's wake, they could act with the swiftness of a poisoned arrow, more maiming than the lash from the long whips of Canadian cowboys. Many a time, to demonstrate this power or to experiment with it, he would kill outright a fly, a beetle, a mouse and even at times a cat, the most tenacious and life-clinging animal in the world. He had once remarked to his particular friends that if he were so inclined, under certain conditions, he could kill a man with the very force of his thoughts. Because of this deadly power, if he could free himself when attacked by a feat of bodily strength with his ju-jitsu tricks or some clever strategy, he would avoid directing a harmful thought towards his enemy.

Although of slight build, weighing scarcely 130 lbs, he had amazing strength and knew how to make good and profitable use of it. He could also ride horses with the born ease of a cowboy, shoot with the eye of Locksley and swim like a fish. He had also acquired a high degree of efficiency in changing his appearance at short notice without the help of pigments or other makeup. Few could beat him in the art of disguise. His knowledge of men was wondrously accurate but most surprising was his loving familiarity with birds and animals, however savage or timid they may be.

This man of many parts, into whose inner character we have had a momentary peep, was in fact not a European, but a descendant of the ancient Persians now known as Parsees. Like the majority of Parsees, the westernized idea of justice was firmly implanted in his mind, as were notions of honour and chivalry. During his thirty years' sojourn in this world, he had lived a virtuous life. He rarely drank and never smoked. Another honourable trait of a most commendable nature was his staunchness towards his friends. He was true as steel and went out of his way to help them, even though he had at times suffered most severely. But greater than his bonds of friendship was the tie by which he was attached to his religion and community.

On the question and preservation of the faith of Lord Zoroaster, he was a fanatic. He was willing to sacrifice not just his wealth, if occasion demanded it, but his very life. He never forgave those who insulted his religion, which his Western learning told him was based on the highest practical principles of morals and hygiene. Even western savants, past and present, have acknowledged the reasonable and practical virtue of the Zoroastrian religion.

The chauffeur of the sumptuous car halted at the entrance of *The Graphic*. His master, the young Parsee gentleman, leisurely fixed his monocle in his left eye. He then picked up the hat that was lying beside him and put it on his head. Looking at his reflection in a small mirror, he carefully adjusted his tie. He put his hand in the inner pocket of his coat and, satisfied, smiled. As he alighted from the car after opening it by means of a secret spring, his left eye contracted for just a moment and the fingertips of his right hand vibrated briefly.

Outwardly, he appeared an indulgently dispassionate member of the upper circle of society but the unconscious physical signs betrayed the intense excitement surging deep within him. At the entrance of *The Graphic*, he encountered a uniformed personage who very politely bowed to him with an eye to the main chance. He seemed pleasantly surprised when his palm encountered a full-fledged sovereign. He was all smiles and seemed prepared to put his very important and hard-pressed self entirely at the disposal of Beram, for such was the name of the owner of that beautiful Rolls Royce.

'Hmmm! By the way, my man, will you inform me who has the register of names of contributants here?' Beram inquired as he temptingly fingered another gold coin between the thumb and forefinger of his left hand. He kept his right hand in his trouser pocket lest even this man, on the lowest rung of the ladder, chance to notice the very slight tremble of his fingertips. Beram never left even an insignificant incident to chance. He knew far too well that it is the so-called 'trifles' that often lead a criminal to the gallows.

'Name of what sir?' asked the not-too-overly-intelligent individual, anxious to do the bidding of this fair and noble-hearted stranger without any delay.

'Of contributants, don't you know?' Beram said in irritably lingering tones, 'The Johnnies who write articles and take pictures and send them here'.

'Oh sir! Yes sir! Please step in this way, sir,' replied the other, inclined to kick himself for this show of ignorance as he led the way.

'Wait a moment,' ordered Beram after taking a few steps. 'I suppose I can trust you to go up to the man who has the register and ask him to give you the list of foreign contributors for the month of August. Tell him Mr Jennings ordered you to get it.'

'All right, sir.'

Immediately after the man left on his errand, Beram sauntered over to an inquiry window and asked to be shown the way to Mr Jennings's office.

'Mr Jennings, the subeditor, sir?' replied the man at

the window, 'You walk straight on and then turn right. You will find a name board on the door'.

Beram followed the man's directions. He stood in the passage, seemingly engrossed in examining the book and magazine covers in a pretty showcase. He was scarcely there for three minutes when his uniformed friend came hurrying towards him with a good-sized book tucked under his arm. Beram calmly accepted the book and slipped another gold coin into the fellow's willing hands. Fingering a third coin, he asked the man to stand outside and guard the door and not to allow anybody to enter the room. He then boldly entered Mr Jennings's office unannounced, where he found the worthy deeply engrossed in a pile of papers.

Beram set the book down on a chair and then coolly announced himself. Mr Jennings sat up with an irritated jerk and was on the point of abruptly ordering the intruder out, but checked himself when noting the stranger's aspect and bearing.

'What can I do for you?' asked Jennings, while indicating a chair on the opposite side of the table. 'Please take a seat.'

'I am very sorry to disturb you, Mr Jennings. I owe you an apology for this intrusion but I was informed that you were the person from whom I can get the information I require. It's about the whereabouts of the man who took that delightful photo of the Tower of Silence in Poona.'

'Impossible.' replied Jennings, a little taken aback. 'Your request is simply out of the question. We never divulge the names of our contributors. What's more, I don't know the photographer. Only Mr Stephens, the editor, knows his name,' Jennings said, closely scrutinizing the stranger's face. He had received explicit instructions from the editor not to divulge the name of the photographer and had been warned about Indians willing to resort to violence to get the information. But Jennings was satisfied that the person before him was not an Indian. Perhaps he is a curious Englishman who wants to meet a fellow adventurer to congratulate him on his success after innumerable failed attempts to get a picture of the world's most secretive sight, Jennings thought.

Beram was a past master in reading the minds of others. It did not require much effort on his part to discern that Jennings had deliberately uttered a lie to end the discussion as soon as possible. With a short laugh, Beram complimented the sub-editor for his astute reply. He then continued in graver tones.

'Well, it is exactly as Stephens told me it would be. You are the soul of discretion. You see, I represent the very well known,' Beram fell silent. He hesitated for a moment, before speaking again.

'Mr Jennings, perhaps it would be advisable to ring up Mr Stephens to reassure yourself that I am here on his advice before I proceed with my gruesome tale? It would help to clear the atmosphere, you know.'

'Oh, that's all right,' Jennings murmured, but he nevertheless swung around, picked up the receiver after a tap or two, and put it to his ear.

'Hello, is that you, sir? This is Jennings. You see, sir, I—.'

Suddenly, Jennings shot up from his seat. He felt as if a vital nerve in his neck had been torn out by the screw-like forefinger and thumb of an iron hand. A terrible pain shot through the whole length of his spine, causing him to stand stiffly at attention, not daring to make the slightest movement to avoid the excruciating pain.

Beram deftly caught the falling receiver from Jennings's nerveless fingers with his free hand. Even while executing this act, he managed to complete the unfinished sentence in the exact tones of his victim.

'—wanted to know if you remember the Johnny who sent the Tower of Silence picture to us from India.' Beram asked, mimicking the nasal twang of the sub-editor.

'Oh yes, Jennings. You mean Mr Young of Liverpool whose handiwork was in our August issue. What about him? Any trouble?' The editor asked anxiously.

'It's a bit queer. I'd better come to your office and tell you about it in person. I'll be over in five minutes with the gent who is here with me.' He replaced the receiver on the hook and then turned towards the paralyzed Jennings with a smile.

'I want to show you something.'

Beram put his hand in the inner pocket of his coat and carefully retrieved what was inside. Hanging limply from his fingers was a devilish blue reptile. He advanced and twined it around his horrified victim's neck. As soon as the clammy body touched his skin, Jennings grew dumb with fright. He shut his eyes, fearing that even the movement of his eyelids would prove fatal to his person.

'This experience will last you a lifetime. That is, if you live. If you make the slightest move, that moment could be your last. Monsieur Venom is in a slight stupor caused by the heat of my body, but he will wake up with the slightest vibration. Take a tip. Remain still and it will of its own accord climb down and make its way elsewhere.'

Beram moved towards the chair where the register lay, deftly turned to the index and found the correct page. He jotted down Young's addresses in both India and England, read a short note about him in the margin and then closed the book.

'At last!' he murmured with a gleam in his eye and tingling fingers as he cast one last contemptuous glance at Jennings. 'Goodbye, my sweet friend.'

In the passage, a third sovereign exchanged hands for one last task because Beram did not believe in needless suffering. Once safely out of the room with the information he needed, he sent the man back into Jennings's room on the pretext of retrieving his cigarette case. Then, he walked swiftly out of the building, climbed into the waiting Rolls Royce and was spirited away. His lips curved in an amused smile as he thought about Jennings who would kick himself when he discovered that the dreadful creepy form draped around his neck was as dead as a doornail.

CHAPTER V

Tring… tring… tring…

'Hello! Hello!' Tinker answered the ringing telephone, his face brightening a little. He was not presently involved in any case and was hoping that something thrilling would turn up, perhaps involving a journey that would give him the time of his life.

'Yes, the governor is in. Hold on a moment please'.

Blake looked up inquiringly from the article he was reading about the Baby Aeroplane Competition to be held at Lympne, an airfield close to Folkestone.

'Mr Stephens of *The Graphic* wants you on the telephone rather urgently, sir. He seems to be in a dashed hurry.'

Blake stood up and took the receiver from Tinker's hand.

'Yes? This is Blake. May I—'

A gasp of relief from the other end interrupted him.

'Blake, old chap, are you free for the moment? Can you spare an hour to come over here? It's about Young and the cursed Tower of Silence affair. I wish I had never published the picture. It would be better if we meet. I would rather not speak about it on the phone.'

'Right-o.' Blake said and hung up. 'The Mercedes, Tinker.'

Hearing Blake order him to ready the car, Tinker performed an exuberant dance. To the utter disgust of Pedro, the dog lying peacefully on the floor, he bent down all of a sudden and pulled hard on the poor animal's long ears. He slipped on a coat and peak cap, and bounded out of the room, nearly bumping into the portly form of Mrs Bardell, the housekeeper. Like an eel, he deftly eluded her hands as she tried to grab hold of him. Defiantly snapping his fingers at her, he bolted down the staircase, bringing in his wake a stream of Mrs Bardell's invective.

A few minutes later, he sounded the horn. Blake emerged from the flat and took the wheel. Tinker saw a familiar bulge under his master's coat. As if divining the meaning of his glance, Sexton Blake put a hand in his coat pocket, brought out a small automatic and passed it over to Tinker.

'Anything particularly serious, sir?' Tinker meekly inquired as he toyed with the automatic.

'Can't say, my boy. It's always safer to be on one's guard. I've been called about the Tower of Silence incident.'

Tinker responded with a soft whistle.

'It was highly improper of *The Graphic* to publish that picture. Stephens's action could end in bloodshed. He has endangered not only his own life but the lives of many others. I warned him against such a course and assured him he would be bringing a veritable hornet's nest round his ears. It seems I was right. It's a pity he does not know much about India, and even less about the Parsees.'

'But the Parsees are stubbornly loyal to the British Crown, in spite of intimidations and inducements, is that not so Governor?'

'It scarcely needs denying, my boy. During the present crisis of the anti-British Gandhi movement, the Parsee loyalty to our king is proverbial. But when it comes to religious scruples, they are a thousand times more fanatical than were the Roman Catholics or the Mohammedans some centuries ago. What they resent most is the inquisitive prying presence of aliens in their religious places of worship.'

'And they are only a hundred thousand out of India's three hundred million population?'

'Yes and that's where the credit comes in,' Blake replied.

'Stephens and the bloke who took the picture had better beware.' Tinker said.

Ten minutes later, they were at the offices of *The Graphic*. They alighted and entered the building, met by the same doorkeeper who had received Beram. But he had grown wise by his recent experience and was coldly formal towards them. His standoffish behaviour surprised Blake. Quite peculiar, Blake thought as he made his way to the editor's office, closely followed by Tinker. Fellows of his kind are usually cringing in their behaviour when confronted by well-dressed clients, but this doorkeeper appears to be a singular exception.

The swinging doors of the editor's office opened and shut with great regularity as sub-editors and other assistants came and went. It seemed as if business was going on as usual. Blake entered without troubling to present his card because the editor and he were on the best of terms. Mr Stephens was dictating a note to a very pretty shorthand typist but he dismissed her immediately when he saw Blake. The curt nod of dismissal struck Tinker as undeservedly rude because he had fallen in nose-touch-the-ground worship at first sight of the beauty.

'Thank goodness! You're here at last. Have a seat, Blake, and find a plank somewhere for yourself, my dear Tinker. And Tinker, try and pay attention to what is being said here rather than thinking about my typist, will you?'

Tinker blushed in confusion. He was on the point of retorting when he met the warning glance of his master. Blake knew that Stephens was trying to calm his strained nerves by this passing show of hilarity. When they were all seated, instead of proceeding to tell them what had transpired, Stephens opened a drawer and took out a folded sheet of blotting paper, which he handed to Blake.

'Look at the slip of paper inside the fold, Blake. I have kept it as I found it, to preserve any fingerprints that might give us a lead. It's good to know some of your methods, old chap, particularly at such moments as these. I will tell you how it reached me after you have examined the note.'

As Stephens spoke, he nervously twirled the end of his moustache. Blake opened the fold in the blotting paper and saw it held a neatly worded slip of white paper. Before he commenced to read it, he picked it up at one corner between his first finger and thumb, and held it against the window light to see if he could locate a watermark. The words were few but forceful. Even Blake felt uneasy about the safety of his friend after reading them.

A well-guarded secret of countless ages has been ruthlessly torn from the very grave and given undue publicity, purely for the sake of playing to the gallery. The religious susceptibilities of the Zoroastrians have been most callously trampled upon. Be assured that your heart and those of your colleagues will be as remorselessly torn from your bodies and thrown to the vultures of the very place you have defiled.

When Blake finished reading the note, his eyes moved towards the editor but it was an unconscious stare. His thoughts were riveted elsewhere.

'By Jove, Blake, do you think there is something in it after all?' the editor spoke in measured tones though he was justifiably frightened.

But he got no reply. Blake appeared to be in deep meditation like a crystal gazer. His eyes were open but he saw nothing around him and yet, he seemed to see what others could not. His nostrils quivered as he smelt a delicate whiff of something aromatic, in spite of the thick tobacco smoke from his own briar which he had unconsciously lit without asking his friend's permission. Stephens recalled the prophetic warning Blake had given him the day after *The Graphic* published the picture of the Tower of Silence.

'You will wish you had never done it.'

Watching Blake's strange look after he had read the note was sufficient to give the editor the creeps.

'If I were you, I would not ignore this pretty warning,' Blake spoke just loud enough for his friend to hear, before resuming in his ordinary voice. 'If I remember rightly, when three to four million Hindu and Mohammedan fanatics rose against twenty thousand Parsees, determined to wipe them out for bravely declaring an open policy in favour of the British government, the stand their small community made against the seditious mob was heroic. And their disciplined, generally cool temper only reached the zenith of a hot burning passion when the non-cooperators, on the strength of numerical force, not only shamelessly molested their women on the open road, but actually tried to raid and defile the Zoroastrian temples. Not caring a farthing for their wealth, their belongings or even their lives, this small handful of Parsees served the practical purpose of a well-trained British battalion. They taught their engulfing sister communities such a terrible lesson it would not be forgotten for many generations to come. The Amritsar-Lahore affair would have been a second Indian Mutiny with all its consequent horrors, were it not for the defeats the movement suffered at the hands of the loyal Parsees in Bombay.'

'By Jove!' Stephens exclaimed.

'You may be surprised to hear that by bringing into play their highly developed mental science, some personages of this unique community well-nigh forced the prime mover to stop the excesses by threatening to exercise their hidden powers.'

'Which if he had not wisely done, he would have been an inhabitant of quite another world?' Tinker interjected.

'Quite right, and no wonder. Their centuries-old practice has endowed them with an unfathomable, mysterious power, which happily they only use in rectifying a wrong, as strictly enjoined by their prophet Zoroaster.'

'Something like white magic, eh!' said the editor, now quite alarmed. 'Blake, old man. I'm glad I have you on my side. Leastways, I feel that you will somehow or other upturn their applecart.'

'Never fear. I will try my best. I already have a clue to work upon. Now please give me a detailed explanation of how you came to be in possession of this disconcerting message?'

Stephens related the whole incident about the daring and clever way by which Beram extracted the name of the photographer from him after hoodwinking Jennings.

'This note was found in the register and these are the three sovereigns he gave the porter.' Stephens handed the items to Blake who pocketed them without a glance.

'The dead snake around Jennings's neck proves my estimate of the Parsee character,' Blake said after listening to the whole story in silence. 'If only I could come face-to-face with Beram, I might arrive at some understanding with him. As it is, we have lost much valuable time. Who knows what other developments have taken place elsewhere. These people take their time making elaborate preparations, but once they begin to act, they would rather abandon their scheme than allow the grass to grow under their feet.'

While voicing these thoughts, Blake was aimlessly scribbling on the blotting paper in his hand. Nearing the end of his speech, he leaned forward and gently pushed the paper onto his friend's desk. He made a sign for Stephens to read the message that he had written in Pitman's shorthand as he continued his conversation.

'Can you inform me who else besides Young took part in this business? It would be prudent to warn them of the danger.'

Stephens played his part. He casually reached out and read the note, pretending to do so in an absentminded manner.

'Please say the name of the chemical expert James Martin, and any other three bogus names of people from other countries that may strike your fancy in audible tones.'

Blake had his notebook ready to record the names and addresses of each party that the editor gave out in a loud and clear voice. He then retrieved his hat and shook hands with Stephens, slipping another note into the editor's hand as he did so.

'You may go home, Tinker,' Blake said as he left the room, seemingly in a hurry.

'Don't go yet Tinker. I want you to ....' Blake heard Stephens speaking to his assistant and knew Tinker would get the note with instructions from the editor. Tinker darted a quick look at the note and let out a soft whistle. It read,

> Disguise yourself. Put on that small moustache of yours and a coat and hat from somebody here. Then come straight to Cartier's where I will make a pretence of purchasing something while I wait for you. Follow any man from *The Graphic* office who shadows me and stick to him like glue. Be very careful. So long.

CHAPTER VI

A large Mercedes stood near the entrance of *The Graphic*. There was no chauffeur sitting at the wheel nor was one standing beside it. Parked on the left side of the road, it was out of the way of the traffic. An urchin with a bundle of papers under his arm was shouting out the latest entry in the coming Baby Aeroplane Competition at Lympne.

He stopped near the car, offering a copy of the paper to people coming and going out of *The Graphic* building.

'Noo hentri at the airplane competition, noo hentri … i … i … i …,' piped the shrill voice.

A few minutes later a lorry was seen approaching. It stopped beside the beautiful car, blocking it from the public gaze. Something appeared to be wrong with the engine because the driver jumped down from his seat with a frown on his face and lifted up the hood, seemingly engrossed in locating the problem. The urchin moved towards the lorry. He looked wistfully at the man who had such a huge vehicle completely in his charge, as if envying his ability to both drive and repair it. Anyone looking at his hunger-pinched face would have felt that the boy's ambition in life was to become a successful mechanic. Standing as he was between the lorry and the Mercedes, he was hidden from view.

He then acted in a curious manner. After opening the door of the Mercedes at the same instant as the lorry engine thundered to life, he slipped in quietly, closed the door after him, and fell flat on the mat below. He then squeezed himself along with his bundle of unsold papers into the hollow incline of the back seat and lay down, concealed by the embroidered flap.

No sooner was this manoeuvre complete than Sexton Blake came out in a hurry from the offices of *The Graphic* and took his seat at the wheel. The car glided smoothly away with a musical purr. Blake stopped at Cartier's Provision Stores, alighted from the car and hurried into the premises. At the counter, he ordered a pound of highly concentrated meat lozenges in four quarter-pound packets. When the bundles were neatly tied up in flat waterproof oblong coverings, he placed them in four different pockets. He then ordered sardines, cheese, sauce, sausages and assorted biscuits to be delivered to his Baker Street address.

On requesting the use of a phone, he was conducted to the empty office of the proprietor, who was also the manager. Once he was alone, instead of using the phone, he opened a door on the opposite wall of the entrance by pressing a secret spring. In the room beyond, he saw his old friend Cartier quietly enjoying a smoke, with an iced drink at his elbow awaiting his pleasure.

'Hello Blakie!' Cartier cried out, jumping to his feet and nearly upsetting the dainty teapoy on which the glass and a bottle stood. 'It's ages since I last saw you. Now that you are here, catch me if I let you off in a hurry.'

'Steady there, Cartier. It's business that has driven me here today. Very urgent business. I hope you have not been monkeying with my wardrobe.'

Blake entered yet another chamber, a luxuriously furnished bedroom and study combined, where he had his cupboard. It contained an up-to-date set of assorted disguises and dresses to effect a complete change of appearance. He had set up this affair at Cartier's to use in times of emergency.

From the bottom panel, he fished out a pair of decent looking boots, an exact copy of the ones he was wearing. He then proceeded to cut the laces of his boots with his penknife to save time and doffed the other pair.

When he returned to the room where he first found Cartier, he found his friend pacing the floor in deep disgust for being deprived of the benefit of his company. Blake patted him on the shoulder, whispered something in his ear and then quickly left him.

On re-entering the store, he saw that the salesman was still occupied with packing his order. He left the provision store, and walked back to his car. Before climbing in, he saw a passerby make a secret signal and knew that Tinker had not failed him.

CHAPTER VII

No sooner had Blake entered Cartier's Provision Stores than the urchin concealed in the rear cautiously cracked open the door and peeped out. Assured that he was not being observed, he boldly stood up in the car and began rubbing something off the window screen with a piece of cloth. He now assumed the role of a motor cleaner to perfection. Passersby scarcely paid any attention to him as he fussed about the car. The boy then opened a highly polished box that was fitted at the corner of the front seat and set about manipulating the machinery with a knowing touch.

The machine worked with the aid of a headgear, which after it was worn, allowed messages to be silently sent and received. The boy managed this with so great a skill that within a few minutes he had done the needful. Then he nonchalantly took a cigarette from a case, lit it and sauntered away to a restaurant on the other side of the road.

Five minutes later, a taxi with a passenger arrived on the scene and took its position along with other cars before Cartier's stores. The occupant remained seated in the car smoking as he apparently waited for somebody. Immediately after, Tinker arrived on foot. He paused for a moment as if admiring the beautiful lines of Blake's car. During that brief inspection, from the disturbed marks, he could tell that someone had recently occupied the rear portion of the car.

As Tinker was turning around, he saw his master approaching the car from the entrance of Cartier Stores. Without turning around, Tinker walked away but he used a sign whereby Blake instantly recognized him.

After Blake drove away at high speed, Tinker saw a taxi start off in pursuit. As it drove past, he saw the anxious face of the single occupant and knew he was the man his master wanted followed.

He had just signalled to his taxi driver when he saw Cartier nodding at him familiarly. Tinker was forced to make a quick decision. He knew that if his master had wanted him to follow his shadower, he would have driven off at a slower pace, giving him time to follow instead of driving away at a furious speed. So, after jotting down the number of the taxi that had followed in Blake's wake, Tinker crossed the street and cordially shook hands with Cartier, who had a message for him from Blake.

'You are to mark the man's face and then await your master's arrival at Charing Cross for the 2:30 for Liverpool. If you see the same man, stick to him. In the meantime, Blake will lead him a merry dance, take his grub at Majesty's and then drive to the station.' Cartier said in a rush. Tinker sauntered away after bidding adieu to the proprietor, got back into his taxi and ordered the driver to take him to a well-known restaurant in the vicinity of Charing Cross station.

At 2.15 p.m., after eating his meal, Tinker posted himself at the ticket office and bought a first class return ticket for Liverpool. At exactly 2.27 p.m., Blake entered the station, rushed to the ticket office and demanded a single for Liverpool in a loud voice. He then ran to catch the train that was due to start in a minute or two. No sooner had Blake left when another well-dressed person rushed to the ticket office window. He put a note on the counter, demanding the same ticket that his friend had just bought, and telling the ticket office clerk to keep the change.

The train was just due to move when Blake entered a first class compartment. Blake's pursuer nearly stumbled against Tinker in his haste to catch the train. The ruse had succeeded. Tinker not only saw that the man was evidently pursuing his master but he recognized him as the person who had followed Blake in a taxi from Cartier Stores.

The pursuer ran, with Tinker at his heels, and two other passengers who were also late in catching the same train unconsciously helped to make things appear more natural. All four jumped into the now moving train. Blake's pursuer and the two others rushed into a first class compartment, while Tinker wisely climbed into one that was second class.

The merry chase then began in earnest. They were traveling the north-western line and a tedious journey of more than nine hours awaited them. The train would pass through Rugby, Stafford and Crewe. After that, it was Blake's intention to run straight to Manchester and from there, take a forty-five minute branch line to Liverpool.

They reached Manchester at 11 p.m. On the station platform, Blake's shadower emboldened himself for surety's sake and stuck closely at his heels. When Blake stepped into a taxi and asked the driver to take him to the Western Hotel, he was within earshot. The man hired another taxi but he gave the driver an address in tones so low that Tinker was unable to hear what he said.

Tinker, to sort out the matter and to avoid following his prey in the dark streets in yet another taxi, quietly climbed into the same one as the shadower. He slid into the front seat beside the driver and shoved a coin into his palm, along with a warning squeeze on the knee to keep mum. Blake's shadower, thinking that Tinker was an acquaintance of the driver, was not alarmed.

CHAPTER VIII

Immediately after breakfast, Blake made his way to Mr Young's house. He had made this journey from London to warn Young about the danger he faced. If he was away from England, Blake knew that he could elicit information from Young's wife about her husband's whereabouts only by making a personal visit.

At the same time he wished to confirm if he was being shadowed or not. He had brought the whole of his experience into play to put Tinker on his shadower's track without the man being aware that his movements were being watched.

At Young's flat, he mounted the stairs and saw the nameplate bearing the young aviator's name. He pressed his finger on the electric button of the call bell. He expected to hear the bell ring but no sound reached him. Thinking that the bell might have a connection in the kitchen, he patiently waited for a full minute. He was on the point of using the knocker when the door suddenly opened inwards. A man barrelled through, butting right into the surprised detective, knocking the wind out of him for a moment. Blake was between the man and the door. In a trice, he found himself twisted round with his back pressed against the door.

He had scarcely recovered his breath when a hand shoved him in the chest. Then with one sudden, swift and lightning-like jerk he felt himself bodily lifted from the ground in the most surprising manner and thrown headlong through the open doorway against someone rushing fast in his direction.

The effect may be better imagined than described. The manoeuvre of so skilful and daring a nature took but two seconds, but the effect was electric. Blake fell in one great dead heap against an aristocratic-looking individual with a monocle in his left eye, who helped to drastically flatten the already snub-nose of a person following close behind.

A faint purr of a powerful engine told them that Beram had escaped. After washing their hands and faces and tidying themselves, the group repaired to the hall, where formal introductions took place. Besides Blake, the party consisted of Mrs Young, her mother-in-law, the great French aviator Maneyrol and a Belgian who styled himself Baron De Latternlove. The two men were on a brief morning visit. Maneyrol was due to take part in the Baby-Aeroplane Competition at Lympne as was the Belgian who intended to participate in the competition in his own machine, Goncelet.

Latternlove had been in India on a short visit to his friend Young. He had returned with a message for his friend's wife and the negative of a very rare picture taken in India by Young. The picture was to be delivered to the safekeeping of their mutual friend Maneyrol.

The men seemed more surprised than pained by their experience until Blake made them realize the great danger in which they stood, particularly Mr Young. Blake was informed that Mr Young was away in India in a town called Allahabad, where the Indian government was experimenting and observing things through aeroplanes, for which purpose a special aerodrome had been built.

After some refreshments, Blake heard what had transpired. Shortly after the two aviators arrived, just when the negative was produced for Mrs Young's inspection, someone jumped from behind the curtain, snatched it out of her hand and rushed towards the exit, with the result that was known to them all. After hearing their tale, Sexton Blake asked their permission to examine the window to discover how the intruder had entered the house.

To help him in his deductions, he asked them to sit in the same positions they were in at the time of the attack. He then repaired to the window and stood behind the curtain to find the peephole through which the intruder had observed things in the hall. It was then that Blake was struck by the astuteness and reasoning power of the man.

In a slit made between the seams of the curtain was stuck a tiny, folded, oblong-shaped note. Blake read its contents with mixed feelings.

I knew you were on my track after the very informative conversation you had with the editor. I was so sure of your coming here that I penned this note in London. Beram.

Blake then turned the note over to further examine it, and saw the following lines hastily written in pencil.

'I saw you arrive outside. By now, you must be standing before the door. If I were you, I would protect these silly idiots. B.'

Blake assiduously sniffed the note like a bloodhound. Satisfied, he quietly slipped it in his pocket book without showing it to the others in the room. He proceeded to examine the floor that was clear and bright with not a speck of dust upon it. Near the window, he saw a cigar end of a particular Belgium make that had been stubbed out by somebody's foot. From the imprint upon that cigar end, a cigar probably smoked by Latternlove, he deduced the intruder had entered from the window by climbing the pipe.

'Mr Blake, I was put on my guard by Young. I took the precaution to get Maneyrol to hide...' The Baron moved his chair closer and spoke in a confiding manner.

'Hush,' Blake interrupted but his warning was not heeded.

'.... the original negative is in a safe place where it will never be found.' The Baron completed his sentence. Blake was sure his shadower had overheard what had been said. The mischief was done.

After warning them in a subdued voice to overhaul and test their machines before every flight in the competition, Blake prepared to take his leave. But before departing, he assured the now thoroughly frightened ladies that the Parsees were chivalrous people and they would rather cut their right hands than molest helpless women.

CHAPTER IX

In a specially decorated and tastefully furnished room in a small private hotel situated at 94/96 Inverness Road, Beram was seated in a deep, comfortable chair. His feet were resting on a footstool. Leaning back with eyelids half-closed, he appeared to be either half-asleep or pondering some very intricate problem.

On separate teapoys on either side of him rested two tumblers containing a punch made to his own taste, with just twenty per cent of rich brandy to give it a delicate flavour. There also rested two tiny jars, each containing the most exquisitely salted Indian tamarind and delicate strips of raw Bombay mangoes.

Having tumblers of punch on two teapoys saved him from any disturbance whilst thinking, being within easy reach of either hand. He chose a piece of tamarind from the jar with great care and deliberation and popped it in his mouth. He found it helpful to do something mechanical with his hands, mouth or feet when he was thinking. At times, he would draw artistic designs on a piece of paper, keeping his eyes glued on their execution as if nothing else occupied his thoughts. But his mind would be hard at work throughout the process, solving an unusually difficult problem.

This British detective Blake was a man of action and intelligence, Beram thought. It was better not to underestimate him. It would be prudent to take precautions against such an astute and powerful foe. While pursuing such a great cause, he could not afford to ignore the capabilities even of a lesser man than he.

If Maneyrol had hidden the original negative, he had to form some plan to get it. Beram stood up, carefully selected a piece of preserve, put it in his mouth and silently paced up and down in deep thought, with his hands clasped behind his back.

Thus half an hour had passed when the door silently opened and an admirably trained little monkey bounded into the room, perched lightly on his shoulder and handed him a slip of paper. It contained the London address of Maneyrol, found by one of Beram's agents.

> Monsieur S.T. Maneyrol
> Worland Hotel Room No-50,
> Oxford Street.

Hearing a soft whistle, the monkey jumped lightly to the ground and bounded out of the room. Beram sent out a signal for his many spies to file their reports in verbature and learnt from them that Tinker was still following his man who was sidetracking Blake.

Beram knew that Blake was smart enough to foresee his plans. Placing himself in Blake's shoes, he knew Blake would not immediately pounce upon the man sidetracking him because he would never divulge Beram's whereabouts.

If I were head detective, Beram thought, I would have the movements of the man himself watched by Tinker on the off-chance that he would lead the way to a rendezvous or be indiscreet enough to send a letter, telegraph or phone in his reports. If Tinker could be engaged in such a fruitless task, Beram could easily track Blake down through Tinker.

After summoning his trusted lieutenants and giving them detailed instructions, as well as explaining his plans to enable them to carry on the work unhampered even if he were incapacitated, Beram courteously dismissed them. The discipline that Beram maintained among his staff was perfect. Though all of them were well-educated, belonged to the rich aristocratic class and were highly influential persons in India and on the continent, when it came to the issue of so vital a nature, all treated him as their undisputed superior, even the two or three relatives who were ripe in age.

As part of the plan, a quantity of luggage was dispatched to the railway terminus, from whence it was to be delivered to the hotel occupied by Maneyrol as if it had just arrived on the London Express. A room facing that of Maneyrol's was booked for Beram by telephone and it now only remained for him to start at the scheduled time.

CHAPTER X

It was the 12 October 1923, the third day of the 'Air Babies' competition, the Lympne Baby Aeroplane Competition. The longest distance, exceeding eighty miles on one gallon of petrol, had already been established by an English pilot, who seemed favoured to win the £500 Duke of Southerland prize.

Now the air was surcharged with excitement among the multitude of onlookers to witness the contest for altitude. The French pilot Maneyrol, the winner of the Daily Mail prize in 1922, had reached an altitude of ten thousand feet. When he came down, he was greeted with a lusty cheer, for the public, to whatever country it belonged, applauds deserving individuals whether the victors be of their own nationality or of a different clime.

In the midst of the throbbing crowd, a man of athletic build with an iron-gray moustache dressed in military uniform was taking a keen interest in Maneyrol's flight. He seemed to breathe a sigh of relief on seeing the Frenchman land without any mishap. Maneyrol was soon surrounded by a wave of congratulations from sportsmen and friends and even strangers who took the opportunity to shake his hand.

'Well-done, mon cheri. I don't think even Percy can do it better,' said a beaming English friend of Maneyrol's named Craft, who had entered into the most cordial relations with the Frenchman during their brief stay together at the same hotel.

'Ah! I am not so sure of it, Craft, my dear fellow,' answered the Frenchman in good humour, 'Percy and Hammersley have something of your bulldog tenacity in them. I don't think I would rest easy until they have had their try.'

Craft had no more opportunity to say anything else to his new friend who was now surrounded by reporters and cameramen. Meanwhile, the military man seemed to lose all interest in the competition and began to drift aimlessly in the throng. He did not even look up on hearing the crowd roar when another miniature machine went up into the air. Instead, his full attention was devoted to the printed list of entries that he had pulled out of his pocket.

Sexton Blake, for it was indeed he, determined by reading the list of entries that Baron De Latternlove would board his machine in an hour and a half. He began to push his way purposefully through the enthusiastic throng, pretending that he had some urgent task to perform to see if anybody was still following him. The Parsee was as cunning as they make them, Blake thought. He had made no attempt to put Tinker off the track. In fact, it was possible Tinker was being led into an ambush with a view to either capture him, or lead him as far as possible so he could not file timely reports.

Blake then noticed his Scotland Yard friend, Inspector Harker, in the crowd. He gave instructions to him to arrest the man who was following him on some pretext. If Tinker made his appearance, the man was to be set free after due apologies. However, if Tinker did not show up, the man was to remain behind bars. Harker nodded and fulfilled his role admirably and efficiently.

When Blake was certain that he was free of his pursuer, and getting increasingly anxious about Tinker's safety, he caught hold of a lad of about eighteen years and gave him a half sovereign with a note to the provision merchant Cartier, with instructions to deliver it post haste. The note read:

> Send four tame mongoose to my flat and place one each in the drawing room and the bedrooms. If Tinker gets in touch, ask him to stop following his man and return to Baker Street to await further orders.

CHAPTER XI

Maneyrol was greatly disappointed when the English pilots Percy and Hammersley succeeded in breaking his record. The knowledge that he had lost the prize was a blow that was hard for his sensitive nature to bear.

Observing Maneyrol's disappointment, Craft suggested that he consider making a second attempt. The Frenchman caught at the idea, ready to risk a second attempt on the exhausted machine rather than live with the shame of a defeat. In spite of the warnings of his other friends and admirers, he went up again in his frail little machine. As was expected, he made a heroic attempt and was seen steadily climbing up into the thin air.

Just then, someone gently pressed the fingers of Craft's left hand, greeting him with a casual remark about Maneyrol's chance of success. When Craft was left alone, his brow wrinkled and the pupil of his left eye contracted ever so slightly. The news he had just received was worrisome. His adversary had executed a clever move by having the man following Blake arrested.

It was time. Time to personally put this meddlesome detective out of the way.

Beram, who had disguised himself as the English aviation enthusiast Craft, had only to wait for the right opportunity to put his plans in action. It was a fight between two mighty intellects: the accomplished product of the West versus an equally accomplished and keen intelligence of the East. One was the champion of righting wrongs through legal channels. The other was out to avenge the wrongs inflicted upon his community. The detective Sexton Blake was safeguarding the lives of those who had committed an awful act against a loyal community. Beram was determined to avenge the unforgivable insult to his religion that was dearer to him than life itself, ready to strike terror in the hearts of any adventurer contemplating a similar feat. Let ethics, law and religion decide who is in the right. Much could be said on both sides, nevertheless it is not our business to say it. Now, back to our tale.

Beram could see the plane piloted by Maneyrol grow larger as he came in to land. A hoarse shout of admiration from thousands of throats acknowledged the nerve of the little man for making a second attempt to regain his prize. Down it came and further down, till it was but two thousand feet from the ground. The roar of the crowd increased as the machine came nearer and nearer at every second.

Now it was at one thousand feet, then eight hundred, now five hundred. Then a gentle ascent before it dropped again to two hundred feet. When it was but a hundred feet from the ground, a deafening cheer burst forth from the crowd who tossed their sticks, umbrellas and hats into the air, waving their coats and hands.

Then, horror of horrors. As if to mock their welcome, the wings of the tiny machine folded together like those of a huge bird swooping down upon its prey. The frail craft crashed down on the hard ground. The happy enthusiasm turned into a deep tragic wail. Doctors and spectators rushed upon the scene and gathered in stunned disbelief around the dead pilot.

But the competition went on, ignoring the tragedy. Beram had thought Maneyrol would survive the crash, at least for a time. He had hoped that, under the guise of a sincere and well-meaning friend, he would have an opportunity to gain the confidence of the injured man and ferret out the whereabouts of the negative. But the death of Maneyrol changed everything. Blake would expect Beram to pay a hurried visit to Maneyrol's flat in search of the negative. To put him on the wrong scent, Beram conceived a daring plot to capture the detective and get him out of the way.

To outwit Blake, Beram needed to find the Baron. He spotted him paying his last respects to his dead friend Maneyrol just before venturing upon the dangerous climb himself. The Baron's heart was heavy and he had lost all stomach for the contest. Beram approached him, and taking him aside, whispered into his ears. The effect on the Baron was electric.

Beram was a man who would rather have as many strings to his bow as possible. Taking all circumstances and unforeseen contingencies into consideration, he had prepared a plan of escape in case he was caught napping in the hotel where Maneyrol had stayed. Money was not a problem. He had a huge fund at his command. Without exaggeration, he had ready cash at his disposal that was fit for a king's ransom and ten times that sum in securities and the rarest jewels. It was therefore no hard task for him to bribe an Englishman to take his place in Maneyrol's hotel if the need ever arose.

He identified an individual of his build with features resembling his own. Then, what nature lacked was made up for by skilful disguise, an art in which Beram was an expert. The resemblance was so perfect that even his followers could not have told the difference if they stood side by side. But they were aware of the deception because Beram kept them well informed about his plans and actions. His foresight and expenditure on his substitution was a good investment. He had another card up his sleeve with which he felt sure he could trap the detective, if all other devices failed.

When he had left the chit for Blake in the slit of the curtain at Young's house, he had scented it, with fractional care, with the bittersweet smell of a very rare perfume of the East. Only the hint of an odour remained whose presence only a trained detective would notice. The chit delivered to the editor of *The Graphic*, the one that had filled Blake with dread, had been doctored by Beram in the same manner.

Beram sensed his opportunity now. His best chance of getting in touch with Blake would be at the aerodrome.

He knew the detective was present among the throng gathered around the dead body of Maneyrol. All that was required was for Beram to offer himself as bait and Blake could be led to his doom. But first he passed some rapid instructions in a sign language of the East to his chief assistant. It was a long message, but both the receiver and the sender were adept at the game and to them it was as easy as holding a verbal conversation. They could have as easily carried out a conversation through the pure medium of thoughts, namely telepathy.

Beram took out a tiny, flat vial from his pocket book, no thicker than a shilling. He opened the stopper and then closed it again without using its contents, returning it to his pocket book which he stowed away in the inner pocket of his coat. After a minute or two, a faint odour of the exhilarating, sweet smell of a rare eastern perfume stole out.

Sexton Blake was occupied in inspecting Maneyrol's body to determine if he was a victim of foul play. But everything seemed to be as expected following such an accident. He was inclined to believe that the aviator's death was accidental, an outcome of a zeal for the aeronautical honour so dear to him. Then the sweet scent wafted across his face and was inhaled by his sensitive nostrils. It immediately stuck a chord in his memory. He had come across it somewhere, but for a moment he could not place it.

Then, memory struck him with the force of a hammer. He could scarcely allow himself to believe his good fortune. It was too good to be true. Was it possible that the prime source of all their worries was in the vicinity? Nevertheless, something troubled the detective. An inner voice cautioned him, but cold logical reasoning quelled any sense of discomfort. Beggars could not be choosers. He must not allow to escape what had come to him by such happy chance. It was a moment for swift action.

'How I wish Tinker were here,' Blake muttered under his breath.

Sheer force of habit drew his mind to work upon the new clue. He was dealing with a cunning person, well equipped with all the accomplishments of the West but flavoured with the subtlety of the East. Partly by reasoning and partly by the process of elimination, he spotted his man. With great care and precision, he noted his height, built and manner of conversation. He recognized him as the man who had drawn the Baron aside and whispered something in his ear that had visibly agitated the latter.

Beram was sure the detective would take the bait. To hide his excitement, Beram caught hold of a stranger and chatted with him in so warm a manner it was as if he were his fast friend. The stranger reciprocated in as verbose a manner, which culminated in their leaving the place together to go to Maneyrol's hotel. The detective, now sure of his man, followed in his wake. Beram climbed into his car along with his new acquaintance while Blake followed in his Mercedes.

At the hotel, when the two men he was after had gone up in the lift, Blake questioned the clerk at the counter. He learnt that one of the men, named Craft, was staying at the hotel in Room 25 and was on very friendly terms with both the Baron and Maneyrol. Blake knew he had to act swiftly. He summoned the manager, and asked for his help. He made a lightning change to his appearance so that he looked like one of the many waiters.

No sooner was his task complete than the front desk received a call from Room 25 requesting that a cup of tea and a black coffee be sent to the room, along with the train timetable. When he entered the room with the order, Blake found Beram and his newfound friend stretched out on easy chairs, amiably smoking and chatting.

After giving one gentleman a cup of tea, Blake placed the coffee cup at Beram's elbow and handed him the timetable.

'I intend to start tonight for Liverpool. My luggage is to be forwarded to Hotel Cecil. Also, ask them to send up my bill in full. I will be going out to make some purchases and will return within an hour or two. Please keep everything ready.' As Beram spoke, the coffee cup in his hand shook slightly.

Curious, thought Blake, noting the tremor before bowing and leaving the room. Blake waited until he saw the two men walk out of the hotel before returning to Room 25. He congratulated himself on so easy a find. The fact that the man known as Craft lived in a room just opposite to Maneyrol's set all his doubts at rest. It was difficult to rely solely on a whiff of perfume to prove his identity because no matter how rare, the use of a scent could not be the monopoly of only one man.

Blake was misled by a psychological factor that was current in the mental workings of even clever criminals. No astute criminal, being fully conscious of Blake's well-known detective skills, would deliberately put himself in the detective's path but Beram played upon this very reasoning by the detective.

Beram knew that to succeed in his vital cause it was necessary to analyse the workings of Blake's mind to anticipate his movements and actions, and then upend the applecart. Beram was sure that Blake was unaware he had been tricked into following 'Craft' and his friend from the air show to the hotel. But he was determined to be cautious.

Entering the room, Blake softly shut and locked the door behind him to guard against a surprise attack. He wanted to find out why Craft was visiting Liverpool and whether he intended to return to Young's house. He looked for the train timetable and flipped through it until he saw an indentation of a nail on 'Liverpool' and 'Marseilles'. Against Marseilles, he saw some figures which he carefully memorized.

Next, he turned his attention to the writing desk. As he was flipping through some papers, a small oblong piece of blotting paper fluttered to the ground. In blotted purple ink were words printed in the tiniest and most pretty handwriting he had ever seen. He guessed it was a page from Craft's diary. The print was not very clear and some words overlapped. It was only when he held it up to a mirror that he could read it.

FrenchyX
BelgeX
Young
Martin (Chemist)
Mongini of Italy
Wilson of America
Herr Steele
Stephens

The names against five, six and seven were the three bogus names he had asked the editor of *The Graphic* to say out loud. His foresight had proved to be of no small consequence. Seeing the cross against Maneyrol's name, Blake believed the death of the aviator was not an accident but a consequence of a diabolical plot by Craft.

The cross against 'Belge' led him to wonder if the Belgian Baron was also in danger. By already placing a cross against 'Belge', it was possible that Craft had left the hotel to fulfil a sinister plan. Perhaps there was time to save the Baron. Blake was now fearful that the Baron's machine had been tampered with as well.

But if Maneyrol's machine was tampered with, why did it not crash on his first attempt in the air? Perhaps it was done only after the Frenchman's decision to make another go of it because the second flight would make a mechanical failure appear to be more natural.

Although Blake was anxious to leave the room to warn the Baron to be on his guard, he knew that a similar opportunity might never present itself again. He decided to make a hurried search to see if he could find the secret address of this man in London and India. In his haste, he drew the blotting pad that was lying on the writing desk towards him.

No sooner was it shifted from its place than a tiny poisonous black adder slid out and, in the twinkling of an eye, inflicted a series of venomous stings on Blake's glove-covered hands. Blake's life would scarcely have had a moment's purchase if he had not taken this precaution. Before he could recover from the shock, the reptile had slithered away and hidden itself. On examining the back of the blotting pad, he found a roughly prepared niche where the snake had been concealed.

Turning his attention to the top sheet of the blotting pad, he found what he had sought. He knew that Craft was not novice enough to blot important letters on a hotel pad. Instead, he was looking for the indentation of pencil marks. From his wallet, he drew out a powder packet and proceeded to sprinkle and shake the contents over the pad. The blackish powder showed in rough outline the indentations of a note. It read as follows.

Urgent
Nowroji – Put – Assam – Burma
Will arrive s/s Hymalya mind the Young kid. – Beram.

Blake could not understand the exact meaning of the word starting with 'Put…' and decided he needed to consult the books in his flat. Blake was pleased that Craft had made a blunder that even an ordinary criminal would be ashamed to admit to. Criminals always overlook the petty facts that lead to their undoing, he thought. The reference to Young was an astounding discovery. It seemed that luck was on his side for once. He replaced the pad but tilted it slightly by inserting a penknife under it so the adder could return.

Blake was elated, but was extremely anxious for the Baron's safety. He rushed to the door, removing his gloves. He tugged the door handle but it failed to open. Looking down with a puzzled frown, he noticed that the finely polished bolt had slipped down into a socket attached to the sill. He stooped down to pull it up. He had to exert some pressure, as it appeared to be tightly jammed into the socket.

'Curious,' muttered Blake.

While pulling it up by his index finger, something pricked him but he ignored it because he was already thinking of how to word the message he would send to the Baron from his car radio. As he stood up and cracked open the door with a curse on his lips for this unwarrantable delay, his right arm fell down in a dead weight at his side. His right temple became numb, as if struck by a heavy blow. The blood seemed to congeal in his veins and he would have fallen to the ground if someone had not caught hold of him.

Even in such a precariously helpless state, Blake did not fail to notice that whoever had come to his rescue had done so very gently. When a hand touched his left temple, he felt a peculiar vibrating sensation in the fingers.

CHAPTER XII

In Liverpool, Tinker was seated beside the taxi driver who was taking Blake's shadower to a hotel. It was only by the cool daring of the lad that he was able to follow his mark because the shadower proceeded to direct the driver to make so many twists and turns before arriving at the hotel that it would have thwarted even the most skilful pursuer.

Early the next morning, Tinker espied the man setting off from the hotel. He led Tinker directly to the quarters where Young resided, reaching there about a half hour before Blake. Both men were in time to observe Beram entering Young's home through a window. Later, when Tinker saw Blake knocking on Young's door, the lad did not remain at his viewing post. Instead, he used the opportunity to enter Beram's car that was parked some distance away.

He slipped into the arch of a neighbouring building and made a rapid transformation. He turned his coat inside out, donned a peaked cap and slipped torn, shabby uppers over his clean boots. A dirty muffler over his turned-up coat collar completed the disguise.

Anyone who saw him would scarcely have troubled to cast a second glance at the rough and ready figure. He sauntered to the car and stood beside it, as if hoping to earn a penny or two by opening the car door for its rich occupant. Tinker was confident the owner of the Rolls Royce would beat a hasty retreat once he knew Blake was also in the young aviator's flat.

Just before taking his position, he used the thin razor-sharp blade of his penknife on the rear tyre of the car. After one deft thrust, he adroitly snapped it off its hilt, leaving the blade protruding from the rubber. Tinker knew that the air would remain in the tyre by the force of pressure against the blade as long as the car was still. But a few revolutions of the wheel would displace it and cause the tube to burst.

He was barely a minute at the car when a peculiar shrill whistle sounded and a man dashed pell-mell out of the house and ran straight for the car. No sooner was the man inside than the car leaped forward like a living thing and was soon lost to sight. Tinker then purloined a bicycle that was standing against the wall of a house and rode hard in pursuit of the car, ignoring the voice behind him shouting 'Stop thief'.

As he had expected, the car and its owner were at the repair shop he had remembered seeing a short distance away. Tinker got a good look at the attractive face of the man and even overheard his well-modulated voice when he instructed the mechanic to deliver the car to his London hotel at 94/96 Inverness Road once the new tyre was fitted to the wheel.

If Tinker had any inkling that the man he was following was the arch-mover himself, there might have been a very different turn of events. Nevertheless, Tinker was elated. But nature at times plays curious tricks and indirectly helps those who step outside the pale of human laws. Tinker was so engrossed in his thoughts that, in spite of fair warnings and loud shouts, he blindly stepped into a crossroad. All of a sudden, he was dashed sideways by a runaway horse. The animal, after taking its toll, did not even pause but cantered onwards upon its mad career.

'A clear case of suicide', a gentleman said to his companion as they stood with the crowd of onlookers who had gathered around Tinker's prone body. 'He must have got clear tired of his life.'

Tinker remained unconscious for two days after he was borne to a hospital. The staff took him for a tramp because of the manner of his dress and the lack of any papers that could help identify him. This was because Tinker had learnt from Blake the importance of always living up to an assumed disguise. Hence, fearing it would give the show away if he were caught and searched, and never dreaming he would be in an accident, he had been careful to dispossess himself of any clues proving his identity.

Tinker was thus prevented from conveying the all-important information about the address of the man he had followed, information for which Blake might willingly have paid a small fortune.

CHAPTER XIII

It was in the early afternoon of 11 October that Tinker regained consciousness. Although he was very weak and could scarcely sit up in bed, no bones were broken and the lad's strong constitution helped him recover quickly.

After some hot beef tea the following morning, having sufficiently regained his wits, he set himself thinking about how best to contact Blake. He disclosed his identity to the nurse and enlisted her help to deliver a note to Cartier. Within an hour he received a reply instructing him to go to Blake's chambers and sit tight.

On the morning of the Lympne altitude contest, Tinker did as he was told, despite his strong desire to watch the competition. Orders were orders and his discipline would not allow him to disobey Blake's express wishes. Not knowing when his services would be needed again, he wisely decided to rest instead.

But at 3 p.m. he woke with a start. Some out of the ordinary sound had awakened him. When he looked about him, he was shocked by what he saw on the floor. He was privy to a show rarely spotted by an Englishman:

a fight to the death between a mongoose and a black cobra, a deadly species of snake found in the East. Pedro, poor chap, was cowering in a corner, ears flat against his head as he watched the drama unfold. He had none of Tinker's enthusiasm for the sight.

Tinker stared like one mesmerized. It was more thrilling than a football final or a crowded boxing hall. Transfixed, Tinker saw the mongoose was entwined with the reptile that was trying to crush it to death. Watching the snake hiss and spit well nigh congealed the blood in Tinker's veins. The mongoose was writhing and squirming in a furious endeavour to bite off the head of the cobra but the cobra avoided all the moves of the small carnivore with dexterous ease, while at the same time viciously stinging it on the nose, eyes, ears and belly.

They were swirling about in a deadly embrace when, with lightning speed and unerring aim, the mongoose snapped at the neck of the snake just below the head. It held fast until the reptile uncoiled itself. Only then did the mongoose let go, after one last vigorous shake.

Tinker could scarcely breathe because the snake now slithered about, bent on escape. With one great spring, it came in Tinker's direction. He shrank further into the wall like a frightened child. With another spring, it struck itself with a sickening thud against the wall, just below the windowsill. Unable to find any purchase, it fell back to the floor. The agile mongoose was instantly upon it but the reptile managed to wriggle away. It regained the centre of the room where it stood upon its tail, swaying defiantly with its fangs exposed, ready for the last great battle. Undeterred, the mongoose launched itself in attack. The sound of the reptile as it lashed about the floor was like a cracking whip. Finally, it wrapped its tail round the leg of a chair and in its death agony, turned the chair over like a ninepin.

The triumphant mongoose, all covered with blood, betook itself to a box placed under the bed. The snake was still wriggling in pulsating fits and starts, as if sobbing, though Tinker saw that it was missing its head. Relieved that the fight was over, Tinker thanked his lucky stars for the foresight of his master.

Feeling sufficiently revived, Tinker searched the house to see if Blake had left any further written instructions. Pedro stuck to his side like a burr, too terrified to venture through the rooms on his own. What Tinker found instead of a message was a mongoose with a bloody mouth in three other rooms. When six o'clock came and went with no word, Tinker was quite uneasy but he did not stir for fear that he might miss Blake. Then, as the clock struck 7 p.m., a pale and despondent Baron De Latternlove was announced by Mrs Bardell.

'Mr Tinker, I believe? Is Mr Blake in?' The Baron asked anxiously.

Hearing Tinker's reply in the negative, he became very agitated, pacing the floor of the drawing room like a caged animal. All of a sudden, he seemed to come to a decision. After acquainting Tinker with the events of the day, he related the message he had received from

Craft at the aerodrome, one that he had hoped to give in person to Blake. When the Baron described Craft's physical appearance, Tinker was sure it was the same man he had followed from Liverpool.

'So you think your flying machine was meddled with by one of those chaps from India, like Maneyrol's? And you think Mr Blake's life is in danger?'

'Yes. They will leave no stone unturned until they find that negative they are after. If they have not already made an attack, they will surely do so soon,' the Belgian replied.

'They have done so already,' Tinker said and then told him about the cobra and mongoose.

'So more than one snake was released in this flat. The bloody state of the other three mongooses is sufficient proof of that. They must have this house under surveillance and will know that I am here. If they see me leave unharmed, they will know their dastardly plan did not work. But if they are led to believe that the snakes have done the needful, they may force their way in. We need to prepare for an attack.'

Shortly after, they heard somebody climbing stealthily up the stairs. The Baron and Tinker quickly took their places. If was a relief to Tinker that Mrs Bardell had left for the night and would not suffer any harm. The door of the drawing room opened slowly by degrees. The intruder hesitated at the door but the sight of the Baron lying prone on the floor seemed to reassure him. He immediately stepped into the room and drew a vial from his pocket. He uncorked the vial and then forced drops of the fluid into the Baron's mouth.

The intruder then began to search the room rapidly and methodically. Locks, even the safe, succumbed in seconds to his touch. While the man was thus engaged, Tinker stole down the service stairs. He held the street door ajar, thrust his hand out and made a beckoning gesture, before retreating behind a pillar. In seconds, someone pushed the front door open and entered. Sure that this person too was under orders from the Parsee, Tinker led him into the kitchen where, all of a sudden, he stooped down and caught hold of the man's ankles in a ju-jitsu jerk that Blake had taught him.

Before he could scream, Tinker clamped one hand over the man's mouth and one on his throat. Within seconds, the man had lost consciousness. Tinker tied his hands and legs like a trussed-up fowl, with a gag over his mouth and left Pedro standing guard. Tinker returned stealthily upstairs where he observed the man he had followed from Liverpool, known to the Baron as Mr Craft, expertly searching the room, the Baron still lying prone on the floor.

Tinker coolly stepped into the room with a revolver levelled straight at the intruder, knowing the Baron would come to his assistance when called upon to do so, as they had planned.

'Very glad to make your acquaintance, Mr Craft. I shall be much obliged if you would immediately raise your hands. I will not hesitate to shoot you for the foul murder you have committed.'

'Well, I must admit you have taken me by surprise, whoever you may be,' Beram replied. He gazed at the person holding the gun, somewhat puzzled, till a note of recognition crept into his eyes.

'The indomitable Tinker, I believe. How do you do? Compliments of the season, sweet lad. But you are wrong, you know. I have not committed any murder. Not yet, anyway.'

'Here, we'll have none of your tricks. Hands up or I shoot. Baron, you can get up now and secure this slippery gentleman.'

But the Baron did not respond. Tinker felt a qualm of fear, thinking that Craft had killed him when he detected the Baron was shamming.

'No need to worry, my friend. He will recover. I gave him a powerful antidote for the snakebite.' Beram said reassuringly.

'What! He was only feigning. You've killed him with your so-called antidote.' Tinker was aghast and his finger quivered dangerously on the trigger.

Beram seemed nonplussed at this news. He knew the gravity of being accused and implicated in the death of a man in England but the seriousness of his position only served to make him more calm and collected. Regardless of Tinker and his gun, he immediately knelt beside the Baron. With cool deliberation, he extracted a wriggling reptile from one of his pockets. Holding it by the neck, he made it sting the wrist of the seemingly lifeless Baron. He then returned the snake to its home and slowly rose to his feet.

'It's all right, Tinker. I have him covered,' Tinker heard a voice that filled him with relief. It was that of his beloved master.

In that fraction of a moment when he lowered is guard, something rushed at Tinker. He was lifted high up in the air, swung around in a semicircle, and thrown against the mantelpiece, knocking the clock and other articles down on the ground with a crash. When he sat up, he saw that Craft had disappeared. The man was a rare ventriloquist, Tinker thought. He had really believed it was his master speaking.

Just then, the Baron groaned. Despite his own bruises, Tinker turned all his attention to helping him stand up.

CHAPTER XIV

At 10 p.m. that night, a cordon of police was drawn around the hotel at 94/96 Inverness Road. Tinker had decided to enlist the help of Scotland Yard after he had spoken to the manager of the hotel where Maneyrol and 'Craft' had taken rooms.

Tinker was afraid that his master had met with foul play because surely he would otherwise have followed Craft when the latter paid a visit to Blake's flat. Also, the ease and daring of Craft's entrance and escape made Tinker positive that he thought himself immune from pursuit by Blake. Not knowing the Parsees intimately, he believed them to be as hard-hearted as the other classes of Indians.

To play a lone hand against such adversaries, without asking for help from the authorities, could endanger his master's safety. But though the police searched high and low, the birds had flown. Not a trace of the Parsees was left. In desperation, Tinker decided to unleash Pedro. With a whoop and a bark, Pedro shot into the hotel. He dashed from room to room, his nose pressed to the floor until he came to the room the hotel proprietor said had been occupied by Craft.

Evidence of a hurried exit was noticeable in Craft's room, with some parcels, boxes and bundles left behind. Tinker now noticed that Pedro was acting in a curious manner. He stood before a rolled-up Indian carpet in the corner and let out a long-drawn wail. Standing on his hind legs, he began to furiously scratch at the bundle with his paws, as if his very life depended upon it.

Believing that Pedro wanted to pursue something behind the rug, Tinker tugged at the carpet but the roll was unusually heavy. Pedro's excitement grew but instead of going around it, he began tearing at the carpet with renewed vigour. Considering his purposeful behaviour, Tinker bent down and untied the strings. Placing his heels firmly on the outer edge, Tinker unrolled the carpet and was astonished to find his beloved master gagged and securely bound inside. Once the bonds were cut off and the gag removed, Tinker was relieved to find that Blake was otherwise unharmed.

'Thanks, my boy,' Blake said.

'The rotters. If it had not been for Pedro, you may never have been found.'

'How did you find this place, Tinker?' inquired Blake.

'Have something hot to drink first, governor.'

Blake was burning with impatience to hear the account, but he allowed Tinker to have his way, just to humour the lad.

CHAPTER XV

'Phew! That was a narrow shave,' muttered Beram to himself before he popped a delicate slice of mango preserve into his mouth.

He wondered how the police had discovered his retreat. It was fortunate that he had obeyed his inner voice and abandoned the premises. He was satisfied that his carpet experiment had gone down well. Blake's earlier capture in the hotel room had gone off without a hitch and his subsequent rescue through the agency of Tinker would appear very believable. Now, all he had to do was wait for Blake to follow the false clues left on the blotting pad of the supposed telegram and the list of names.

Tinker was sure to tell Blake about the Baron and the snake venom, and Blake was already convinced that Beram had engineered Maneyrol's death. He would believe Beram had fled the country to evade arrest for the Frenchman's murder and to kill Young. Once on his trail, Beram would make the detective follow him to Burma, where he would give him the slip. With Blake safely out of the way in Burma, Beram would have a free hand to recover the negative and all the copies.

Beram got up, selected a piece of tamarind preserve, and began pacing the length of the deeply carpeted floor. A few minutes later, he sprawled on a rich Persian rug made of silk, with his head resting on a bundle of Lahore shawls. He would teach the Europeans what it meant to trade upon the religious secrets of a loyal sect that did not harm them either by deed or word.

As Beram had planned, Blake did bite the cleverly prepared bait. He did his work carefully, looking up first the destination of the 'SS Hymalya' and then losing no time in booking a passage on a different Italian ship. It would arrive in Bombay one day ahead of the *SS Himalaya*.

CHAPTER XVI

The *SS Himalaya* docked at Ballard pier in the Bombay harbour at the scheduled time of seven in the morning. There was the typical bustle, rush and excitement. Passengers descended the gangway and luggage was brought down on the backs of porters. After the usual formalities, the passengers drifted away with their belongings in cars, taxis or victorias.

Trevor, a dupe disguised as Beram, was accosted by a Parsee with an obsequious and respectful demeanour. A sigh of relief escaped Trevor as he took his seat in a private car as the Parsee gentleman gave instructions in an ostentatious manner to the porter carrying the luggage.

'How did you fare during the voyage, Mr Trevor? Any signs of being followed? Did anyone try to force his acquaintance upon you?'

'Not that I know of. I freely mixed with the passengers and afforded every opportunity for such advances.'

'That's where you are mistaken. You do not know this man. He is already here and has seen you arrive and even knows we are in this car. To trace a man's movements, it is not necessary to be near him. If the destination is known, you can even be ahead of him. That coolie who trampled on your toe with that heavy load upon his back was none other than Blake.'

'By Jove!' Trevor said.

'He is staying at the Taj Mahal Hotel. He arrived last night on the *SS Himalya*. If you look back, you will observe a taxi following us and another behind it. Which of the two is following us, I cannot say. Perhaps both of them are, to make sure they succeed.'

'Why not trap him here in Bombay and detain him instead of going to Burma,' Trevor suggested.

'Orders are orders, my friend. Perform your work like an automatic machine and don't think at all. Earn your monies, and go home.'

'If you think a nigger can threaten me with impunity, well...,' spluttered Trevor, hot blood rushing to his cheeks and temples.

'Shut up, you ignorant fool,' the Parsee gentleman said, utter contempt showing in his face. 'First of all, Parsees are not niggers. It is our misfortune that we have to eke out our existence in India, far away from Persia, the land of our birth. We are descendants of those Persians who 7000 years ago had a mightier sway over the world than you Britishers will ever have. Now, let's turn to business. You promised to do a certain thing in return for a princely fee. For now, you are a mere hireling and must obey your masters. Put that in your pipe and smoke it.'

The words were spoken in so deliberate a manner that the Englishman was taken aback. He had never imagined there could be so great a spirit and power of language and logic in a native of India, about whom he was led to think from his school days in contemptuous terms.

'Oh, keep your wool on, you savage,' said Trevor with a frightened laugh. 'My mistake. I own it.'

Trevor's companion was right about Blake. He was in Bombay and had been disguised as a coolie at the port.

'Curious,' Blake murmured, as he sat smoking in a comfortable deep chair. He recalled the look on the face of the man he had believed was Beram when he arrived. It was not that of a man returning to familiar surroundings. He had observed all the facial expressions of his object and was now trying to analyse their meaning. While he was in deep meditation, he heard a tap on the door and a waiter approached saying he had visitors. They were the two taxi drivers commissioned to observe the movements of Beram after he arrived in Bombay.

'Now relate what you saw in detail and don't omit a single point, however trivial it may appear to you,' said Blake to Peter, the taxi driver who was a native Christian.

'An unexpected thing happened, sir, which greatly facilitated my work. From the turns the car took, I felt sure they suspected we were following them. So I overtook them and recognized their driver who is a friend of mine. I will meet him today at a gambling den. Once I had decided that, I left Ganesh to complete the task.'

'Well done. Write down the name of the owner of the car, his address and occupation and that of the driver. Also write the name of the gambling den.' Then Blake turned to Ganesh, the second driver. 'Now let's hear your story, my man.'

'I followed the car as directed. When we came to the base of Hanging Gardens, I saw Peter overtake their car and continue towards Peddar Road,' Ganesh said, indicating the exact locality on the map of Bombay that Blake had spread on the table.

'The car I was following took a left turn towards Nepean Sea Road. It disappeared in the compound of bungalow no. 8. I thought that was the end of it, but then I saw that the car had dashed out of the other gate, minus one occupant. In my haste to turn around, there was a minor accident. The remaining occupant got out and threatened to take proceedings against me for rash driving. He sent his driver to call for the police. I was a bit scared. The police are more inclined to do justice to their own pockets than to the poor public. Hearing my entreaties, he led me inside the bungalow. Then the gentleman caught hold of my shoulders with both hands, looked straight in my eyes and abruptly asked me to make a clean breast of it. Nothing loath, I gave your exact description and told them that it was you who asked me to tail them.'

'How did they take it? Please be precise.'

'They were alarmed. They held a hurried whispered conversation. Then one of them promised to let me off if I undertook not to mention this incident to you. As I was leaving, a fifty rupee note was pressed into my hands.'

'Good, good, very good,' Blake said encouragingly, 'but still…'

He then paid them for their services without completing his thought, ordering them to answer his call any hour of the day.

When he was alone, Blake rushed to his dressing room. He performed a change, now looking exactly like the driver Ganesh. He walked out of the hotel and hailed a passing taxi, avoiding one from the common stand. He asked the driver to stop some distance away from the bungalow on Nepean Sea Road and told him to keep the engine running, paying him more than his legitimate fare. Blake proceeded confidently to the bungalow and entered without even ringing the bell. But he found the house empty. He searched the place from top to bottom and even called out loudly, but it was deserted.

Blake had lost Beram's trail.

Chapter XVII

'That was a quick change. I never dreamt that in actual life one could move quicker than we do in the theatrical world,' remarked Trevor, who was in comfortable loose garments and reclining on an easy chair.

'You have not seen anything yet. Blake will be a little surprised at our showing a clean pair of heels,' said Rustom, for that was the name of Trevor's Parsee guide and companion, the one who had met him at the harbour.

'Hum,' drawled Trevor sleepily.

'Sleep as much as you can this afternoon, my friend. You will need all your energy in a short time.' Rustom warned. The spider is a bit cautious, but he will walk into the parlour, he thought to himself. Everything had transpired just as Beram had anticipated.

Rustom rang for a domestic and asked him to round up three others. He sent them out with messages either to be delivered personally or by post, telegraph or cable. Then, Rustom completely transformed his own features and looked quite unlike his former self. Before he left, he gave instructions to the servants not to allow Trevor to leave the building until he had returned. He walked for a while and then hailed a victoria.

'Where to, sir?' asked the driver from his coach box.

'Victoria Terminus,' Rustom replied.

After about twenty minutes, they were in a very crowded locality, thickly populated by Parsees. He went to the top flat of an old building with four entrances and then returned to his transport. Arriving at Victoria Terminus, he paid the fare, sauntered to the station bookstall, purchased a copy of the *Times of India* and carefully began to scan its pages. All along, he kept watch and when he was satisfied with his observation, he stepped into the telephone box nearby.

'Hello! It's me. Where is our Joe at present?'

'Padu, the man who was on watch, says he entered the Nepean Sea Road bungalow disguised as Ganesh.'

'How many men have you deployed to keep a watch on him?'

'Five men.'

'Alright. Photograph our Joe in his latest disguise and send the photo along with Adi to Reclamation at 7.30 p.m. sharp. Reserve a table at Greens for 7:45 p.m. Keep watch to see if he follows us from Greens. I will have to ring you later. Someone is waiting outside to use the phone.'

Rustom hung up and went to the offices of the Bombay Theatre opposite the railway station where he purchased four front row tickets. Then he stepped into the telephone booth and called to complete his instructions.

'If our Joe goes to the railway station, our man stationed there should do the needful. But if he drives to the aerodrome at Santa Cruz, let him be. Do you follow?'

Rustom then walked for twenty minutes to the B.A.C.P.R. station at Church Gate. He boarded a local train to Bandra. There he got into a waiting car and was whisked away.

In the meantime, Trevor was sipping a cup of tea, listening to some records that had captured the voice of Beram and was closely studying a variety of photographs of his subject. While Beram was a liberal paymaster, he did not tolerate mistakes made by those who served him. But Beram had carefully chosen his man because Trevor was an actor of no mean ability. He was feeling refreshed after his nap when he received a note with instructions for that evening.

Rustom returned to pick him up and both men were driven to Reclamation. They had barely arrived when a man approached their car and handed Rustom a photograph. They then drove to Greens restaurant, adjacent to the Taj Mahal Hotel. A waiter obsequiously showed them to their table. To all appearances, they were there to enjoy their drinks and the delightful music, greeting acquaintances who stopped by their table. After paying their bill, they were driven away into the starry night of an Indian summer.

Blake was pleasantly surprised when he saw the pair enter. Remaining outwardly calm, he did some quick mental calculations. After his fruitless search of the house on Nepean Sea Road, he had gone to Messrs Thomas Cook & Son, Hornby Road, where he left certain instructions. Next he went to the Army & Navy stores where he made some purchases. Retiring to the lavatory, he quickly transformed himself with makeup and the Parsee long coat he had bought.

Thus free from the fear of being followed, Blake went to Greens. From sheer habit, he sat in his disguise at his usual table at Greens. When he spotted Trevor and Rustom, he was confident their presence there did not indicate they were following him. But when Blake walked out and recognized Beram's car, he saw the driver did not fit the description given to him by Peter. Although Blake knew Beram's ultimate destination was Putao in Burma, he wanted to discover all he could. Perhaps luck or a small indiscretion would lead him to their secret meeting places or their working methods. He had not heard from Young in Allahabad and wondered if the telegram he had sent had been intercepted. The Parsees appeared to have unlimited resources and seemed to possess a mentality that could win by lengths against the inherent subtlety of the Chinese, even after giving points. But curiously, they also had a chivalrous instinct like the knights of old.

Along with their psychological powers, deep learning and noble disposition that was the outcome of their oldest traditions, the Parsees had a mine of wealth. For how else could so small a number hold its own against 300 million in this land of mystery and mighty upheavals? Seeing there was nothing much to lose and more to gain, Blake went straight to Beram's car and whispered something in the driver's ear.

The driver started the engine and brought the car under a lamp post. He then climbed upon the hood and closed off the gas jet. No sooner had they been plunged in darkness than Blake landed an uppercut and a blow to the pit of the drivers stomach. The driver crumpled without a sound. After hurriedly donning the driver's uniform, Blake poured out the contents of a brandy flask on the prone man and left him on the wayside to be spotted by a constable and run-in for being drunk.

He drove the car back to its original position and calmly waited for Trevor and Rustom to come out of the restaurant.

'Adi, drive straight to the bungalow on Nepean Sea Road and then to our aeroplane shed. Then return to the bungalow and remain there until you get a message from Calcutta,' Rustom said to Trevor. As the car started moving, he whispered to Trevor, 'It's Blake, right enough. He's caught the bait.'

Blake had already decided on a plan of action when the car reached the Nepean Sea Road bungalow. As Trevor and Rustom began walking towards it, Blake swiftly ran between them, caught hold of their heads and brought them forcefully together. Taking immediate advantage of their temporary helplessness, he removed the papers and a purse from their pockets, and drove away before they knew what had happened.

'By Jove, hot stuff that,' Trevor said when he could

gather up his thoughts. 'You seem to have miscalculated, my dear fellow.'

'Not at all,' said Rustom. 'I expected something like it.'

'Well, really!' Trevor said, sounding annoyed as he rubbed the tender lump on the side of his head. 'Look here, old boy, the next time you expect such a reception, you may consider giving me a straight tip beforehand.'

Chapter XVIII

In the brief period since Blake's arrival in Bombay, a whirlwind of developments had taken place. Sitting on an easy chair in a different room in the Taj Mahal Hotel under another name, he had debated whether to proceed to Putao before the Parsees or go to Allahabad. If he could verify that Young was safe in Allahabad, he would not need to go to Putao. But what if Young had already been kidnapped and taken to Putao?

Blake grew tense when he heard a knock at his door. He slipped his hand into his pant pocket and wrapped his fingers around a small but highly serviceable revolver. But it turned out to be a waiter, bearing a telegram on a tray. It was a reply from Allahabad, sent in care of Mr Balance of the firm T.C. & S. who had told the night watchman to immediately deliver any urgent messages to Blake.

'Observer Young was posted to Rawalpindi. Sustained serious injuries in an aeroplane crash. Was removed to hospital, but has disappeared.'

That settled it for Blake. It was clear that Young had been spirited away to Burma. He was up against a community with a highly developed intellect, a liberal education and a rigid sense of honour and respect for their religion, their prophet and Dadar Hormuzd (God). He knew he was risking his life by going to Putao but there was no way around it. He would have to take his chances.

CHAPTER XIX

Putao district is situated on the Burma-Assam border, roughly some 2000 miles from Bombay, a journey that takes three nights and two days by train. It is a very backward district where slavery still exists, though the British Government is doing everything it can to suppress it.

The Naga Hills of Putao district, an unadministered area, has grown notorious for the human sacrifice. Those sacrificed are chiefly Nagas purchased from the neighbouring head-hunting villages.

In a hut in one of those villages, a man was securely tied to a pole. From sheer fatigue, hunger and thirst, the captive could scarcely keep himself erect. When he did manage to raise his head, in spite of the grime and dust that covered his features, it was possible to see he was a white man. A stream of natives poured in through one door and went out the other to view this miserable creature and gloat over his capture. To offer a white man to their gods was an opportunity of a lifetime, a sacred trust that had fallen into their hands. It appeared that nothing could save him, for these savages were prepared to give up their lives to propitiate their gods who might otherwise unleash unspeakable calamities and misery upon them.

Blake had come to this sorry pass because he had journeyed to Putao disguised as a Burman without taking anyone into his confidence, lest the Parsees got an inkling of his movements. He reached Calcutta by rail in a third class compartment. He then got aboard a coastal steamer to Rangoon. From Rangoon, he proceeded to the interior towards Putao by joining a group of mendicants, men who live by alms and wander all over Burma, India and Ceylon.

When they arrived, Blake was tired and dusty. His companions did not appear to feel the strain, perhaps being habituated to this way of life, and fell at once to lighting fires to cook rice and fish in clay utensils. After their meal, they smoked ganja in their chillums before falling asleep outside the mandir.

Blake followed their example, but not before giving a silent secret signal to a particular beggar. Early the next morning, Blake and his companion set out ostensibly to seek alms. His companion made inquiries at every home where they begged. They found out that a white man had been seen the day before and that he had been observed entering a hut some distance away. Blake heaved a sigh of relief that he had found Young's trail so soon.

They began walking at a pace that would appear unusually fast to the local gentry. They approached the hut boldly as if to beg for alms. Going around the hut, they found a man sleeping with his back to the thatched door. Blake stealthily approached him and gripped his neck in his strong fingers, instantly choking the cry that almost escaped the bewildered sentinel's lips.

After securing him with a rope, Blake pushed the door open and entered the hut while his companion stood watch outside. When Blake flashed the light of his electric torch around the dark interior, he saw a form trussed like a fowl lying on the ground. Blake recognized Young at once from the photograph he had seen in England.

Just as he removed the gag from Young's mouth, he heard the hoot of an owl, the agreed upon warning signal. Blake switched off the torch and drew Young close to the door.

'Stand on that side and take this,' Blake said, handing Young his revolver. 'If need be, don't hesitate to shoot.'

The door opened and several men rushed through with burning torches in their hands. Blake, who was quickly hemmed in, realized they were outnumbered.

'Shoot man, shoot,' Blake cried, but no shot rang out.

The man he had left guarding the door had taken to his heels after giving him the warning sign. With his hands now securely tied behind his back, Blake was hauled up and taken outside. Of the four men standing before him, Blake recognized one instantly as Rustom, the man who had met Trevor when he landed in Bombay on the *SS Himalaya*. The man who Blake had presumed was Young stood free.

'The disguise is a clever one indeed, but I want to see if the paint comes off. Bring some water and wash his face with this handkerchief.' Rustom ordered.

When the dye did not come off Blake's face after some rubbing the captors looked uneasy. Then Rustom tore off the button of Blake's shirt and laid his chest bare. It was also brown and resisted all efforts to rub the colour off. Next Rustom took out a penknife and catching hold of Blake's thumb, scraped vigorously at the nail. Rustom's persistence paid off when the flesh under the scraped nail appeared pink.

'A walnut stain. Very clever, my friend. But with all due deference to your reputation, Mr Blake, your methods of detection are amateurish,' said Rustom, making Blake wince. 'Immediately after you knocked our heads together at the Napean Sea Road bungalow, Beram ordered me to accompany this gentleman posing as Mr Young to Burma, to receive you with open arms and give you the welcome you deserve. We spread the news of a white man being held here for your benefit.'

Rustom whistled and in response a group of natives entered. After speaking to them in their dialect, Rustom turned to Blake and told him that it was imperative for him to remain where he was till their plans were complete.

'Tomorrow you will be sold as a slave by public auction. Of course, your liberty will be repurchased by us after some time. I feel sorry for you, but drastic times require drastic measures.'

The Parsees departed and Blake was left alone at the mercy of the natives. The next day he was sold by auction. The purchaser had to promise that Blake would be kept as a slave for at least one year before he was either sacrificed or sold to anyone else. But the wretched man did not keep his promise. When a man from the Naga Hills offered him a large sum of money, he succumbed to greed.

And so it came to pass that Blake was staked out in the sun awaiting his fate. His plight was now serious and it seemed that only a miracle could save him. So great was the superstitious dread that the new slave owner felt about this special sacrifice that he was determined not to release him for love or money.

CHAPTER XX

Mr Thornton, the commissioner for the North East Frontier, reached Putao just after Blake was sold.

He had been appointed by the Government of India to stop the slave traffic at Putao and to do away with the practice of human sacrifice in the Naga Hills. When he heard that an Englishman had been sold by auction, he immediately made inquiries. After no small amount of trouble, and after Blake was resold to the Naga tribesman, Thornton caught the man who had first made the highest bid for Blake. After a great deal of alternate coaxing and threats, the man confessed to what he had done.

Thornton saw the seriousness of the situation. He had brought fifty retainers with him to fulfil his mission but he feared that if he made a bold move and marched openly to where Blake was imprisoned, it might only serve to hasten his end. After all, what were their lives and property worth before the dark fury of a disappointed god!

Instead, Thornton planned to rescue Blake with six stalwart men. Two were Englishmen, three were Burmese and one was a man born on the border who was very

familiar with the area. He had been christened Scamp
by Thornton, which he considered a great honour.

'Well, you cannibal. You had better take the lead and
tell us how we should best proceed,' Thornton said to
Scamp in the native's dialect because the only English
word Scamp knew was 'soar', meaning 'sir', which he
used whenever he got the opportunity.

'Blessings of the black-faced god with the yellow tail
and iron claws be on you. There will be no danger until
the moon is full,' Scamp replied. 'It is many miles from
here to their camp and the road is dangerous. But today
there will be no danger because thousands will be going
to see the sacrificial ceremony. It will be safe for us to
join the crowd if we dress like them.'

Thornton had been directed to wipe off the scourge
of human sacrifice and slavery by inducement, empty
threats or other peaceful measures. In cases of extreme
danger to a life, he was entitled to act as he pleased, but
not without his government's sanction. However, there
was no time for that now. He decided to go as a private
adventurer. If blood was shed, he would not be brought
to account for it officially.

He armed his men with service revolvers and
fifty rounds apiece, taking along a spare. Leaving his
subordinate in charge of the rest of his men, Thornton
set off with the team of six selected men, walking
alongside the crowd heading towards the sacrificial spot.
By dusk, they had arrived at the village where Blake was
being held. Along with the others, they also filed past
for a look at the white man. No sooner had they entered

the hut than a commotion arose. A stampede followed and every man jack of them seemed to be caught by an intense wave of anger. So great was the commotion that Blake was quite forgotten.

Taking advantage of the melee, Thornton and his party fell upon the priests as they stood craning their necks to see what was going on. They were swiftly bound, gagged and blindfolded by Thornton's men. Thornton himself cut loose Blake's bounds in the twinkling of an eye but Blake was so weak that he flopped down on the ground in an inert heap.

'Take courage, old man,' whispered Thornton, as he thrust the spare revolver into his hand and a flask of brandy between his teeth.

He thrust a wig of flowing white hair on Blake's head, which the rogues had shaved at sunset, leaving only a tuft in the centre that they had anointed with coconut oil according to their custom. A beard that was already gummed was fixed to his chin and the brownish-yellow flowing robe of a mendicant was slipped over his head. The transformation was completed with ash sprinkled on his face, hair and hands.

Blake's limbs had recovered their circulation and gained strength. One of the two Englishmen had already pinned a prepared parchment on the pole with a dagger. The note read:

'None need follow. The white man is safe. We will die rather than surrender him and allow our God with the black face to be cheated of his due. Signed: Chief of Kantipzain.'

Blake and the rescuers joined the crowd, running alongside, gesticulating wildly and asking what had happened.

'It is a very serious matter, brother,' replied a Mongolian. 'A rescue party is reported to be advancing to free the white man.'

Thornton and his men knew that it was Scamp who had spread the rumour. All of a sudden, the crowd changed direction and rushed towards the hut that had served as Blake's prison.

'Kill him, kill him on the spot,' the crowd chanted.

Blake and Thornton and his men also ran back along with the others so as to appear inconspicuous. The crowd gathered around the hut began drinking the potent locally brewed arak that they had filled in their goatskin water bags.

No sooner had they reached it than a howl of rage emanated from within the hut. The news of Blake's escape reduced the crowd to numb disbelief. Blake, Thornton and the other two Englishmen realized they were in danger of being exposed so they also turned fierce and suspicious looks upon their neighbours. But when the paper pinned to the pole was read, the anger of the crowd abated and the crowd scattered, taking their different ways home. Thus Blake was saved from a terrible fate.

Chapter XXI

Mr Stephens of *The Graphic* lived in a comfortable house surrounded by a well-kept and beautiful garden on Rupert Street in Piccadilly. A select party had gathered to celebrate the birthday of Mary, the editor's wife. Dinner was over and pleasant strains of music floated into the chill air outside where several motor cars of different makes were parked.

The chauffeurs were in the warm kitchen, leaving the cars in the charge of a young boy. Seated in one of his plush charges, he appeared to be enjoying himself, only spoiling the image by frequently looking at a watch that he took out of his pocket. At 10 p.m., he got out of the car, removed a small phial from his coat pocket, and artfully poured a drop or two of the fluid on one tyre of every car, with one exception. He poured the remaining liquid on the roadside, and threw away the bottle. As he slunk back to the car where he had been sitting, he heard the music stop.

Inside the flat, the guests stopped dancing and took their seats around a table. Placed before them were fifteen delicate tumblers of thin clear-cut glass. Mr Stephens rose to speak.

'Ladies and gentleman, allow me to present to you my most worthy and highly esteemed friend Arbab Andishir of Persia. He came to my office a few days ago bearing a letter of introduction from Mr Sexton Blake, a very good friend of mine and a world-renowned detective. I have persuaded him to show us a trick or two. I believe that if Arbab Andishir had been born many centuries ago, he would surely have been hailed a prophet.'

This speech caused a great stir among the guests. They were eager to witness some clever feats, but were surprised by the eulogy from their host, who was known to be highly sceptical in such matters. Arbab Andishir did not appear to feel even a bit nervous at finding himself the object of their intense curiosity. Of the many eminent men and women present, one was a magician who had never failed to dazzle his audience. Two famous experimental psychologists, one of them a theosophist, a learned priest and the famous manager of R- theatre, were there along with the cabinet minister for foreign affairs.

Arbab Andishir rose and approached the table, carrying a bag. It was an oblong affair, supporting a flawless white and finely polished slab of marble on its iron frame. By its side was a silver pail of water, also supported on a triangular iron frame. A tiny silver glass called a loti floated on the surface. When Arbab Andishir took a bundle from the bag, Stephens rose and conducted the Persian to a dressing room. On his return, the guests looked up at Mr Stephens for an explanation, but he studiously avoided saying anything on the subject.

Minutes later, they saw a form approaching wearing wooden sandals and dressed in a long flowing robe of richly embroidered cream silk. He stretched out his hand and took hold of the loti and carefully washed his hands in a basin nearby. He then moved the glass tumblers on to one side of the table and carefully washed the cleared space. Replacing the tumblers on the washed side, he sprinkled water on the remaining portion and cleaned it. He then took the tumblers and washed them one by one with the water from the pail and arranged seven of them like a pyramid, four at the base, two on top of it and one right on top. The remaining eight glasses he put upside down one above the other in two rows on the corner of the table. He then fanned the burning glowing coals in a silver receptacle resting on a tall iron framed teapoy.

After carefully selecting pieces of sandalwood from his bag, he put them on the glowing coals. He then sprinkled a handful of incense in a circle around the coals, releasing a pleasant fragrance. After standing silent for a moment, he turned to the expectant onlookers and honoured them with a courteous bow.

'Ladies and gentleman, in the first place, I have to apologize and ask a thousand pardons for keeping you waiting through these preliminaries. But they are essential to the success of my enterprise. I am a Persian and not a Mohammedan. In fact, I am a Zoroastrian.'

Here Stephens gave a startled look and seemed

deeply agitated, though he tried his best to appear calm. His wife saw the distress on his face but was not unduly alarmed. One other member was greatly surprised, but successfully hid his emotions.

'I see that Mr Stephens seems upset upon hearing the word "Zoroastrian. My esteemed friend Blake had acquainted me with your particular case. He has deputed me to get in touch with you because he has been detained in India.'

The editor of *The Graphic* seemed to relax on hearing this. But Tinker, the man in the audience who had managed to hide his surprise, was not so easily satisfied.

'At the outset, I consider it proper to inform you that the Zoroastrian religion is based on purity, not only of the mind, but also of the body. Only a body cleansed by water and freed of impurities by the fumes rising from the glowing fire can evolve pure and holy thoughts. Thought is the essence of our well-being. Good thoughts lead us to light, whereas evil thoughts drive us away from it. To achieve mental purity, it is imperative to bathe and dress in clean clothes. Underneath this cloak, you will see I wear a clean linen pyjama and a sudreh, a shirt of pure white muslin, over which is a kusti, a string of pure bleached wool wrapped in three folds round my waist, specially prepared by the women of the priestly class of our community.'

He untwisted the knots and removed the string from his waist, placing it in the bag before selecting a fresh one, which he placed about his neck like a shawl.

'With the proper chantings, I will now tie the kusti

around my waist. When I give it a whip-like crack, the glass resting at the top of the pyramid of tumblers will crack in two. This will occur through the deep concentration of my mind achieved by reciting a Zoroastrian prayer. You may ask why a tumbler would crack just by the recitation of an ordinary prayer. The explanation is simple. In the prayer, in the name of the Lord I call upon the evil spirit Angremanio to leave the place where I intend to worship God in peace and quietude. As the evil spirit is all pervasive like the good one, the void felt when Satan departs is marked by the cracking of the topmost tumbler that is situated in a purified place.'

Beram (for it was him) began murmuring his prayers, reverently facing the burning coals. No sooner had he begun his prayer than they glowed with a brilliance that struck awe in the minds of those present. Holding the end of the doubled string in left hand, and the middle of it in his right, with the remaining portion hanging loose in the air, he cracked it with some force whilst murmuring the words 'Hai-re-man-vad-shan,' meaning 'hence Satan'. All seven tumblers rattled on the marble slab. Then the sound of the top glass cracking was heard by all.

'The mind of a human being is as delicate as these glasses, and ten times more responsive and sensitive. If I were to continue, your minds would be filled with that ecstasy which might culminate in a mild insanity. Instead, I will now show you the force of stringed instruments.'

He placed five glasses under the table. With the remaining three, he put two face down on the table and the third face down on the top of them. He tucked a violin under his chin and began playing the instrument. Slowly at first, then gradually he went faster until not only the three glasses, but also the nerves of all those present vibrated with a thrilling sensation.

The spellbound audience were rudely brought back to the present when the topmost glass fell on the marble table and broke into a hundred pieces. Beram was now ready for his final coup. He gave a sign to his man, who began collecting the materials just used.

'I see, ladies and gentleman, that you now believe that I posses supernatural powers. I may even go so far as to say that you will still continue to hear the alluring strains of music, even though it has actually stopped. You are quite asleep, so sound asleep that you cannot wake until five minutes have passed.'

Beram left the room and walked down a corridor, passing several rooms till he stood before a child's cot, where a beautiful golden-haired youngster slept peacefully with the nurse sleeping on an iron cot by his side. Beram gently lifted the child. He then placed an envelope on the cot before swiftly leaving the room. When he returned, all the guests and their hosts were in the same posture as he had left them. Beram wiped his face with his handkerchief and then purposely let it fall to the ground.

He went straight to his car where his chauffeur and the boy were waiting. On taking the driver's seat, he took off his shoes and handed them to the chauffeur who put them on and started walking rapidly away.

CHAPTER XXII

Tinker enjoyed the music played on the violin by the man Mr Stephens had introduced as Arbab Andishir. He found it as captivating as the other guests. It is possible that he too might have passed into a peaceful slumber but the persuasive voice that stole the brains of the others had subconsciously put Tinker on his guard. When he suggested that they were all asleep, Tinker remained wide awake, instead feigning sleep so successfully that even Beram, posing as Arbab Andishir, was reassured.

When Tinker saw Arbab Andishir walk down the corridor, he construed the man's object was to commit a theft. As soon as he was out of sight, Tinker sprang up, grabbed the Persian's coat and stuffed it inside the piano before quickly resuming his position. When the intruder returned and left the house with something tucked under his flowing robes, Tinker followed at a discreet distance. As it was dark and misty, Tinker remained unobserved standing behind a porch pillar. He watched as someone got out of the car and disappeared into the darkness.

Tinker had a choice. Either he could follow the man

on foot or he could follow the car. He chose the latter and darted half bent towards the editor's car which was a high-speed machine, with the added advantage of having a self-starter. He followed the Persian's car, without showing any lights, but had hardly gone a hundred yards when the front left tyre burst with a loud sound and the car skidded onto the side of the road. This alerted Beram to the fact that he had been followed. Were it not for his forethought in doctoring the tyres of all the other cars, all his efforts would have been in vain.

'Baker Street, and drive like the blazes, if you want to earn a quid.' Tinker said to the driver of the passing taxi that he had flagged down.

'Right ho!'

At Baker Street, Tinker ran up the stairs in double quick time. He wrote a hasty note and put it in a book on the shelf. When working on a dangerous case, it was the custom of the detective and his assistant to studiously follow this practice. He then ran downstairs and brought Pedro out of his kennel. The hound was delighted at the prospect of a run and frisked about Tinker like a big awkward pup. Tinker ran back with Pedro to the waiting taxi. Back at Stephens's house, he observed that Mrs Stephens was raving like a mad woman and the editor was pale and quite aghast.

The ladies were trying to sooth his wife Mary, while the men were passing a letter among themselves. The cabinet minister had left after assuring Stephens of his help.

'So he succeeded in eluding you after all,' Stephens said, rushing up to Tinker.

'Have you found any trace of the child, Mr Tinker,' the theosophist asked.

'What child?' Tinker asked.

'My baby,' wailed Mary. 'Oh! Can nothing be done to save my precious child from the clutches of these monsters?'

Tinker spoke reassuringly to the grieving parents before grabbing the circulating letter from the nerveless grasp of Mr Gloat, the magician.

Mr Beram, President of the Special Committee appointed for safeguarding Zoroastrian interests in India, requests the pleasure of the company of Mr J. Stephens Esq, on the anniversary of the day of the PHOTO, to witness the ceremony of his only child being exposed to the gentle mercy of the departed at the Tower of Silence at 12 noon.

P.S. It is open to you to substitute yourself in his place, for which an application should be personally presented the day before at a certain address to be intimated immediately on publishing a notice of request in the *Times of India* newspaper in Bombay.

Tinker recognized two things that almost knocked the wind out of him. One was the handwriting of Beram, and the other was the barely perceptible smell of a scent that Blake had described. He quickly decided to follow the man who had left by foot, as the one in the car had already escaped his grasp. He removed the coat from the piano where he had hidden it and held it up to Pedro's nose. Pedro gave an intelligent woof of joy and virtually dragged Tinker away as he rushed for the door.

Pedro's powers were very keen and the guests present knew to what purpose he was set, but none volunteered to accompany Tinker. Pedro first led Tinker to the spot where Beram's car had been parked and gave a bark of delight at picking up the scent. Tinker had not expected such success for he thought that Beram must have left in the car. But from Pedro's excited behaviour, it now seemed he was the man Tinker had seen leave on foot.

Chapter XXIII

For ten minutes, Pedro was going strong, dragging Tinker behind him. From the renewed excitement of the dog, Tinker concluded that the quarry was near and the trail was coming to an end.

All of a sudden, and without the slightest warning, the hound that but a moment ago had been excitedly tracking the scent collapsed. He writhed a little and then his body lay still. Tinker was altogether distracted by this unexpected calamity and at the helpless condition of his canine friend. He had sense enough to hold his pocket watch before the animal's nose and sighed in relief when he saw that he was still breathing.

When he saw the headlights of an approaching car he did not hesitate to stand in the middle of the road, waving his arms and whistling. His whistle attracted the attention of a policeman, and his added presence in the middle of the road forced the car to stop.

'Look here, you jackanapes,' the driver shouted. 'Can't you find a better way to commit suicide than to bring trouble to honest folks?'

'Hand him over to the policeman,' drawled an irritated voice.

'I suppose you have a wife dying at home and three dozen starving kiddies crying out for bread,' sang out a third.

'Gentlemen, I'd be grateful if you would help me in saving the life of this dog. I beg of you to drive us to the veterinary hospital.'

'But who are you?' the last speaker asked.

'I am Tinker, Sexton Blake's assistant, and this is Pedro, his dog.'

'The nearest hospital is three miles from here. He may succumb on his way there. Why not take him to your den, Jack?' one of the passengers said before turning back to Tinker. 'He is a veterinary surgeon, you see.'

'Oh, very well,' the doctor sighed, already regretting the sacrifice of a jolly night.

The car stopped before a house on Queenly Street. The doctor and his friend then lifted the inert Pedro between them and carried him inside. When Pedro was hoisted up on a large table, the veterinarian named Jack prepared a serum, which he carefully injected into the inner side of Pedro's thigh. From another cupboard, he took out a tumbler and a liqueur bottle, poured a goodly quantity in it and handed it to Tinker.

'Drink this up, my boy! It will smooth your strung nerves. It's a good sign he is still breathing.'

Tinker drank the contents with a gulp and immediately lost consciousness. The hound too was heavily drugged by the injection but Beram, for it was he, took the precaution of tying up the hound with a strong chain.

'Who was it who shot the dart into the hound?' Beram asked.

'It was Tamil Master,' came the answer.

'Well, he did his work perfectly. We have to visit Martin in an hour. Ask Adi to take his car away and tell him I will not need him any more tonight. And tell him to bring the taxi around at noon tomorrow.'

When Beram was alone, he lifted the drugged and bound Tinker and laid him gently on a sofa. He sprinkled some iced water on his face and forced some raw brandy through his clenched teeth. When Tinker came to, he saw Beram pacing with his hands behind his back.

'Where are the negatives?' Beram asked abruptly.

'Find out for yourself.'

'And where is Blake?'

'Where he is,' Tinker retorted.

'I can force you to answer these questions by torturing Pedro. All is fair in love and war.'

Tinker's cheeks grew pale at this threat, but he took courage when he remembered Blake telling him that the Parsees had fully imbibed western culture and that they always honoured the rights of humans and showed kindness towards animals.

'You would never do such a thing,' said Tinker with as much faith as he could muster.

'You are too young to understand human nature, my friend,' Beram replied.

'Ah, but the governor is not.'

'Until now I haven't seen your governor live up to his reputation.'

'Don't crow so soon. You will find yourself at his mercy,' fired back Tinker.

'You saw what I was up to at the Stephens' house and yet you did not intervene. Was it because you were afraid?'

'If I had known you planned to kidnap an innocent child, I wouldn't have hesitated to shoot you,' Tinker said.

'Brave words. By the way, I know where Blake is at present.'

'Where'

'Find out,' Beram replied with a smile.

Then Beram stepped towards Tinker and prodded his neck with a forefinger. Tinker's face distorted with pain and his head fell inert on his chest, his eyes closed and he lost consciousness.

'This time you really are asleep. Now open your eyes, look at me and remember what I say and act in accordance with my orders. Whenever you receive my thought message, no matter where you are, you will obey me and unhesitatingly do as I bid, even against the express command of your master. You will forget everything that has just happened.'

Tinker's eyes opened wide and stared at Beram with fixed intensity.

Slowly, he nodded.

CHAPTER XXIV

Beram's power over animals was unique. Domesticated quadrupeds loved him, however fierce and disinclined they were towards strangers in general. Conscious of this power over the four-footed gentry, Beram decided to take the recuperating Pedro along with him.

Sitting beside the dog in the taxi, Beram gently tapped him on the head and back. Within minutes, Pedro revived. To demonstrate his gratitude, Pedro attempted to cement the friendship by licking Beram's face, but was prevented from doing so out of religious scruples. When they reached house No. 113 on Rampert Row where Martin resided, Beram saw the lights were still on although it was late at night.

Beram, disguised as Blake and accompanied by Pedro, stood at the front door and rang the bell.

'Mr Blake! I thought you were in India,' the Englishman exclaimed.

'I have just returned from India. I have come to pick up the negative. It is not safe to keep it here under the circumstances.'

'Do come in, Mr Blake. Make yourself comfortable. I

had another surprise visitor who was asking for the same thing. I will just run up and fetch the Johnny and leave him in your hands.'

A few minutes later, Martin returned with his visitor.

'Mr Sexton Blake, meet Mr Aspandiar of Calcutta, the famous curio collector. Mr Blake is the famous Baker Street detective you may have heard about.'

Martin's visitors sized each other up as they shook hands.

'I see that you don't remember me, Mr Blake. Not surprising, considering the number of years that have passed. It was a big case in India. You asked me to loan you a cirrus of a particular design to help you solve a case involving a Siamese convict who had escaped from jail.'

'I do remember the case very well but you have the advantage over me, sir.'

'No doubt I am much changed.'

'Perhaps.'

'At the time, you may remember I refused to accept any compensation, though you offered me a very generous sum. You then said that if I ever asked for a favour, you would grant it.'

'I see. You want the negative, don't you?'

'I only want to see the negative of the Tower of Silence photograph, but Martin has refused to oblige.'

'You want to look at it? I don't see why not. Martin, I think we can give Mr Aspandiar a look at the negative.'

'If you say so. Follow me please.'

As Martin led them down the stairs to an underground

vault, Beram thought that Aspandiar's face seemed vaguely familiar. He noted that Pedro had rushed to him with a bark of delight and the man willingly resigned himself to the canine's affections.

'You see the faint outline of a square on the wall there, on a level with your shoulders? The negatives are stowed in there. The aperture can be opened only by a concealed spring. This an opportunity to show off your skills, Mr Blake. Let's see if you can locate it.' Martin said.

Aspandiar also seemed to enter into the spirit of the friendly challenge. Beram silently cursed Martin but maintained his composure. He stood close to the square. After a careful inspection, he pressed down on an almost imperceptible elevation. In a trice, two steel doors flew open from the centre and Beram felt a spurt of liquid gas shoot into his face. He instantly lost consciousness and fell with a thud. A cunningly devised trap door swung open in the floor and Beram was swallowed in the twinkling of an eye.

Aspandiar rushed upstairs and looked out of the window to see if any of Beram's team was outside but all he could see was a taxi. Using the binoculars Martin handed to him, he honed in on the taxi driver and saw that the man was asleep. Meanwhile, Martin had tied a steel anklet around Beram's left ankle and secured it to a ring on the wall with a strong chain. He then emptied the contents of a small phial down the unconscious man's throat and applied strong astringents to his nose.

When Beram came to, the first person he saw was Aspandiar who had returned to the underground vault.

'Liancti kutra. Elke arthoshti thai acomaha kamma elke perjatn'e maded kerta tune sharam nei avti? (You cursed dog. Are you not ashamed to help a nonbeliever in this life and death matter?)'

Aspandiar, none other than Blake in disguise, ignored this outburst. Instead, he wiped off the traces of disguise from his face, put on Beram's coat, and left the room.

'Kem suigioke? What, asleep?' Blake asked the taxi driver in Gujarati as he got into the back seat with Pedro

'Are nahire sahib (oh no, sir).'

'Take me home,' Blake said.

Instead of driving to Baker Street, the driver drew up at a big hotel in the West End and halted there. Blake had never imagined that Beram would stay at a public hotel, but to avoid the driver's suspicions, he coolly got down and boldly went through the entrance after telling the driver to return at seven the next morning.

Blake had no intention of attempting to locate Beram's hotel room because he did not know under what name Beram had registered there. Instead, he hailed a passing taxi and was driven home.

Chapter XXV

After Blake had escaped from the clutches of the Naga Hill savages in Burma, he made a beeline for Rawalpindi. As soon as his train roared into the station, he set out to pay his respects to the political agent. Blake was informed that Young had recovered from his injury and was on the point of being discharged from the hospital to resume his duties at the frontier.

After some discussion, they decided that the safest course would be for Young and Blake to board a special aeroplane and fly first to the continent, before crossing over to England. This was done without a hitch and they safely reached Liverpool with only four refuelling halts. After surrendering the aeroplane to the proper authorities, they paid a brief visit to Young's wife and mother and then boarded a train for London, taking the precaution of travelling in disguise.

With Young safely hidden away, it was time for Blake to visit the chemist Martin, the fourth name on the list Blake had read on the blotting paper pad during the Lympne competition. But within a few minutes of his arrival at Martin's house, someone had knocked at the door. When Martin went to let his second visitor in, Blake retreated into an interior room. When Martin came looking for him, he was surprised to see that Blake had disguised himself as Aspandiar. Blake took the opportunity of imparting the startling information to the latter.

'He's come at last and disguised himself as me.'

'By George, if he had arrived before you did, I might have been duped.'

Blake used his fertile brain and immediately suggested a plan of action that the reader knows was enacted.

When Blake saw Pedro, he grew anxious about Tinker and it made him doubly determined to capture Beram. It was almost 2.30 a.m. before he reached Baker Street, hoping to find Tinker in his bedroom, but it was empty. He then hastened to the spot where communications were secreted when pursuing a difficult case, where he found Tinker's note.

Following a Persian. It's possible he might lead me to Beram's headquarters. Tinker

In spite of his anxiety, Blake knew he could do nothing at the moment. Besides, he had not slept for thirty-six hours and could scarcely keep his eyes open. Tinker might be in need of all of Blake's reasoning powers, but without an hour or two of sleep, he would be of no use. Besides, Beram was safely buried in Martin's vault and posed no threat. The last thing he did just before falling asleep fully clothed was to call the Baron and tell him that he needed to contact Martin urgently.

At 5 a.m., he was startled by an impatient knocking at the front door. Though he had slept for nearly two hours, he felt as if he had lain down but a minute ago. Nevertheless his rigorous and self-imposed training of many years instantly brought him around to face the exigencies of the moment. Obeying his cultivated instinct for safety, he ran into his dressing room and with a few deft touches, transformed into Aspandiar. When he opened the front door, somebody shoved him aside and rushed headlong up the stairs calling out for Tinker.

Not finding him in his room nor in the sitting room, the man was emerging from Blake's bedroom when he came face to face with the disguised detective. Stephens, for it was indeed the editor of *The Graphic*, failed to recognize Blake. He instantly pulled out his automatic and aimed it at the stranger.

'Who are you and what's your business here? I have you covered. If you dare to move as much as an inch, by heavens, I will riddle you through with bullets.'

Blake, being ignorant of the kidnapping of the editor's child, was somewhat taken aback at the reckless attitude of his friend. Seeing the man's nervous condition, he replied in his normal voice.

'Good heavens, Stephens. What's the matter, man? Your face is as white as death.' As Blake spoke, he removed all traces of his disguise. Reassured, Stephens lowered his revolver and rushed to him with outstretched arms.

'Thank god you are here, Blake. But where is Tinker? You do know what happened to my child, don't you?

That beast. If I ever get hold of him, I'll break every bone in his body.'

From Blake's blank stare, Stephens realized he knew nothing about the events of the previous night.

'Calm down, my dear fellow. Take a seat and tell me what happened.'

Much reassured by Blake's calm manner, Stephens related his story, leaving Blake in awe of the daring and clever manipulation, the almost uncanny powers exhibited by the Persian.

'I don't know how Tinker avoided succumbing to his evil influence, Mr Blake. I lost consciousness long before he stopped playing that thrilling music.'

Blake had heard and read much about the Parsees in India from authoritative sources. He had no doubt that the Persian who had performed his tricks to perfection was none other than Beram, the leader of the movement to take revenge on *The Graphic*. He felt a degree of respect for his antagonist and relief that by a rare piece of luck he had him secured at Martin's house.

Blake prepared to leave for the hotel to make some inquiries. But before he set out, he conducted Stephens into his laboratory and gave him a tiny airtight tin box. He explained what was in it and when and how to use it.

After slipping two automatics in his pockets and wrapping Beram's coat in a bundle, Blake set out with Pedro. At the hotel, he met the manager who afforded him every facility after hearing about the activities of Beram and his team. They searched high and low for the child, even enlisting Pedro's help, but all to no avail. Thoroughly frustrated, Blake decided to return to Martin's house.

CHAPTER XXVI

By a curious coincidence, on the previous night, Beram's lieutenant Rustom had just stepped out of the hotel when he saw Adi, Beram's driver, at the wheel of a car, though he did not get a good look at his passenger.

When the heard the soft purr of the returning car, and saw that Adi was now alone, he let out a whistle that was a secret sign. Adi felt a surge of hope. Just moments ago, he had been filled with despair. He had been suspicious about the man who had gotten into his taxi outside Martin's house. To verify his suspicions, he had driven to the West End hotel. When his passenger did not protest, he was convinced it was not his master.

Adi was far too shrewd to halt the car immediately when he heard the secret signal. Rustom raced after the car and jumped in. The car surged forward like a living thing and was soon lost to the sight of any curious observers, stopping only once it was on a deserted street.

'You of all the persons! Here in London! The Lord be praised. He has sent you at so critical a period,' Adi exclaimed.

Before Rustom could respond, a flood of words poured out as Adi related the events of the past night and his fear that Blake had captured Beram. Rustom was horrified when he heard this additional piece of bad news. Surely the man in the car could not be Blake! The latter was safely tucked away in the Naga Hills. When he received an urgent wire that Young had escaped from Putao, Rustom had immediately set off for England to personally inform his chief about this slip. He was fearful that their scheme of vengeance would be wrecked. But like a true Zoroastrian, he instantaneously cooled down and listened carefully to Adi.

'I knew it was not Beram because he asked if I had fallen asleep. Beram would know that I was only shamming. Secondly, he failed to give the code word, the signal we had agreed upon that all was well. Finally, he got out of the car at the West End hotel. He must be congratulating himself for hoodwinking me.'

'Tinker and Stephens's brat are under control, are they?'

'Yes.'

Rustom considered several plans and evaluated the pros and cons of each. His thinking grew more lucid when he realized the enormous responsibility that he now automatically shouldered as the second in command.

'Listen, everything will depend upon the alacrity with which we work. Tinker and the child must be taken to a safe place. Tell Bajon to take them on board the *Mineros*, the yacht we have on hire. It is moored at the Downs, the anchorage between the coast and the

Goodwill Sands. Leave this car for him to use, and bring the Napier here.'

Ten minutes later, they arrived at Rose Cottage, a house with large grounds, surrounded by a beautifully kept garden. After Beram bought the property through an agent, he made several modifications, both to the original structure and the underground. It was now a labyrinth, a network of tunnels and passages.

Adi ran inside to perform his tasks while Rustom summoned a meeting of the council to explain his presence and his plan to rescue Beram. When he was done, it was much admired for its daring and simplicity. There were twenty men who had come to England under the leadership of Beram, though he was too shrewd to have all of them stay at Rose Cottage. They were scattered in batches of twos or threes under different names and guises. Although there was deep consternation on hearing the news about Beram, they believed that Rustom's presence offered a ray of hope.

The council of five were prepared to risk their liberty and even their lives to save Beram because the success of their enterprise depended on him. What were lives, precious as they may be to their influential and wealthy families, in comparison to fulfilling the sacred trust given to them by their co-religionists and their God?

Once they were all ready, the cars whisked them to Martin's house, where they were deposited, waiting along its side streets. Only the car carrying Rustom stationed itself in front of the chemist's house. He got out and knocked loudly on the door.

'Mr Martin, Mr Martin. Quick. Please open the door, in heaven's name,' Rustom shouted out in an urgent and hoarse voice. Martin, still half asleep, raced out of his bedroom and opened the front door.

'Why! What's the mat...' The words were scarcely out of his mouth when he was punched in his chest just below the ribs and then dealt a stinging blow to the right temple that numbed his brain. Momentarily paralysed, he could not shout for help.

Rustom rushed in and furiously shook the inert figure. He helped him sit up against the wall, holding him in that position. He glared into Martin's eyes with the ferocity of a mad animal.

'Sleep.' Rustom said the single word with great intensity. The combination of shock and physical pain made Martin lose his mental balance. This weakened condition gave Rustom the power to put him into an instant trance.

'Tense.' Rustom said, and immediately Martin's body perceptibly stiffened.

'Open your eyes and listen.'

Martin opened his eyes and looked straight at him with a dazed expression.

'Where is Beram?'

'In the cellar.'

'Lead me there immediately.'

Four other Parsees had entered the premises like silent ghosts while Rustom was engaged with Martin. The only other person in the house was the Baron who had arrived post-haste in obedience to Blake's instructions on the phone. Alarmed when he heard the loud knocks on the door, he nimbly leapt out of bed, snatched the revolver from under his pillow and tiptoed on bare feet to Martin's room.

But Martin had already gone to open the front door. The Baron saw the chemist enter the dining room and pass into the adjoining hall through the curtains that partitioned the two rooms. By the time he crept closer to peep through the curtains, Martin was already in a trance. The Baron looked on with growing dread.

Unaware of the four other men who had entered the house, the Baron was sure he could deal with the single stranger. He boldly stepped forward, pointing his revolver straight at Rustom's heart.

'Hands up,' he drawled.

Rustom immediately raised his hands.

'Hands up,' the Baron heard several voices say in unison.

Remembering how Tinker had been hoodwinked by Beram's ventriloquism, he thought this was also such a trick. He did not hesitate to shoot.

A bullet whizzed harmlessly above Rustom who had fallen immediately flat on the floor at the instant the Baron had pressed the trigger. Before the Baron could take a second shot, two forms, as if released from a catapult, flung themselves at him, striking his body.

'Gag and bind him, and hide yourself between the folds of the curtain.' Rustom ordered before darting forward to lock the door and switch off the lights. He then went to Martin and held his hand tightly between his palms.

'Go to your room at once.'

As Martin walked away, there was a rapping at the door.

'Rat-a-tat! Tat! Tat! Rat-a-tat! Tat! Tat!'

Rustom first toppled a chair over before putting on the lights and opening the door.

'Is it about the explosion?' he asked the policeman standing outside. 'I was helping Mr Martin carry out an experiment, when the retort burst. The gas escaped and exploded with a loud bang.'

'It almost sounded like a pistol shot,' murmured the officer.

'Come in if you like and have a look around.'

The policeman took him up on his offer and stepped inside where he was quickly overpowered, gagged and securely bound.

'Where are the keys?' Rustom demanded of Martin.

'Under the carpet near the door.'

'Stand up and take me to the cellar, and be quick about it.' Rustom ordered. He had managed to locate the keys by this time.

Martin took him to the vault and began tugging at an iron ring attached to a trap door. It refused to budge. Rustom pushed him aside when he saw it had a keyhole. The third key he tried was the right one. He pulled at the ring and the door came up smoothly on well-oiled hinges.

'Wait here,' Rustom said to Martin.

He descended the stairs two at a time and jumped several of the last few, just missing Beram. Turning on his torch, he flashed the light against the walls until he found the light switch. He saw Beram furiously tugging at the chain attached to an anklet.

Without a word, Rustom darted forward and knelt before him. Pushing a key of a curious design through a hole in the anklet, he set Beram free.

'Follow me.' Rustom raced up the stairs, closely followed by Beram.

Beram bent down and discovered that the man lying trussed up beside the policeman was the Baron. A couple of the men who had arrived with Rustom carried in sacks of potatoes from the car and emptied them on the floor. The chemist and the Baron, with knees tucked double under them, were shoved into the sacks. Some of the potatoes were thrown in at the top before they were tied up. The sacks were then loaded into the car.

'Take them to the Mineros.' Beram ordered. Adi and four of the men drove off with their captives while Beram and Rustom took their seats in the second car and drove to Rose Cottage.

Chapter XXVII

In a bed-sitting room in Rose Cottage, Beram chose a slice of salted mango from a jar on a teapoy in the centre of the pleasantly warm and well-decorated room. The pictures on the walls were highly suggestive and might have been declared vulgar by a crude mind. But the large carpet covering the floor and the rich silk curtains were of the finest quality and design.

After his brief imprisonment, finding himself in pleasantly familiar surroundings gave peace to Beram's mind.

'Have some. They are quite delicious.' Beram said, waving a slice of mango.

'No thanks. My teeth can't bear it,' Rustom replied.

'Who is this Aspandiar? We have to find out,' Beram said as he flopped down in an armchair beside Rustom. 'The fellow was instrumental in holding me up.'

'I believe it was the man Adi drove to the West End hotel.'

'He appeared to be a Parsee but I can't understand why he would act against us. Blake has chosen the right man for this work.' Beram renewed his attack on the jars of preserves. 'You are quite sure that Blake is secure?'

'Quite sure. I personally saw to that.'

'But it is possible he has escaped. And you have no idea where Young is at present?'

Rustom shook his head, looking extremely dejected. He almost wished for a reprimand from his chief. Even a flogging with a dog whip was preferable to a cynical, contemptuous remark from Beram. But Beram surprised him.

'I have not thanked you yet, Rustom, for the alacrity with which you brought about my release.'

Rustom's eyes gleamed with joy at the praise. Beram knew how to win the hearts of his followers.

'Now leave me to myself for a while, will you. I must think of a way to find out who this fellow Aspandiar is. In the meantime, you are in charge of locating Young. His home is in Liverpool, so you had best start from there.'

He sat thus for five full minutes, and then, getting up, he sprinkled his hands and face with water from a silver loti. Turning to the west and facing a tiny oil lamp, he began unwinding his kusti, and retied it, all the while chanting. When he was done with his prayers, he tried to think of what he would have done in Blake's place.

But he was up against a man who was his equal in analysing the mind of his opponent. Blake, still disguised as Aspandiar, returned to Martin's place. His shock may be better imagined than described. The first sight that greeted him was the prostrate policeman lying securely bound and gagged on the dining table. Blake immediately freed him, upon which he looked at him with venom in his eyes, as if it was he who was the culprit. Blake was in no mood for niceties. He quickly brought the man to his senses by introducing himself. The officer then changed his tune.

'Come, come, my man. Make haste. Tell me what happened, including every simple detail. It may prove to be of great importance.'

The officer of the law related what had occurred, giving a glowing account of his own unprecedented heroism against a gang of savage opponents. After a quick search of the house where he found no clues, Blake wondered if the hotel would be his best bet.

He had hardly taken a dozen steps, when he saw an organ grinder sitting dejectedly on the ground near the gate of a house opposite.

'Like to earn half a quid, what!' Blake asked.

'Whose leg are you pulling, you heathen? You may as well ask whether I would like to smoke good tobacco in this here pipe,' came the response from the none too polite gentleman.

'Where were you last night?' Blake asked, slipping a coin into eager hands.

'I was lying here near the hedge, governor,' the man said with a sudden show of civility.

'Did you notice anything unusual going on in that house opposite?'

'Well now, come to think of it, I thought I heard a pistol shot. No sooner that done, a copper turns up.'

'Has nobody come out since then?'

'I really don't know, governor. I suppose I must have dozed off.' Then, with a gesture as if suddenly remembering something. 'I did hear somebody getting into a car, but I can't say from where he trot out. Funny, I feels as if I heard someone say the word rose.'

'Was there a woman in the car?'

'I couldn't say, governor. It was dark. Maybe it meant his lady love, if not that louse who lives further down.'

Blake's face instantly lit up with hope.

'Look here, my good fellow. Show me the place if you wish to earn another ten shillings.'

'Not I, governor. Not even for twenty quid. I won't bring them folks who help the likes of me into trouble.'

Blake's persuasion and even threats were of no avail. Seeing that the man was determined not to say a word more, Blake once again entered Martin's place. By this time, the freed constable had brought his chief, Inspector Spur, to the scene. The inspector looked at him in surprise, at first not recognising him in his disguise.

Blake whispered something in his ear. Inspector Spur drew aside the curtains, looked out of the window and then turned to nod at Blake. Blake sauntered out past the tramp, who was already preparing to leave the neighbourhood.

Chapter XXVIII

Back in his rooms, Blake called the editor of *The Graphic*. Before embarking upon his scheme, he checked in the mirror to correct his disguise.

Blake was aware of a unique characteristic of the Parsees. A Zoroastrian, to whatever station of life he belonged, could easily distinguish his co-religionist in a crowd. This he is able to do from mannerisms that are so subtle that they cannot be discerned even by the most observant eye of a person of another community.

Blake also took the precaution of taking along some sudrehs in his bag, open at the neck and without any buttons. Sudrehs, pure white shirts made of mulmul, are a necessary adjunct of a Parsee's wardrobe. No matter the clime, he is rarely without these sacred vestments. Due to its colour, it cannot be worn for more than a day or two before getting soiled by dirt and perspiration, thus requiring a change of clothing and automatically preserving the purity of the body. Similarly, all the religious tenets of Zoroaster are based on a principal such as this, serving a practical purpose. It is the reason that Zoroastrianism is an ideal and a perfect religion, based as it is on the belief in one god and the promise of salvation through the universally accepted tenets of Maneshni, Govashni and Kunashni, or good thoughts, good words and good deeds.

Blake was thinking fondly about Tinker, knowing the life of his affectionate assistant depended entirely upon him. If the four men already in the hands of the Parsees were smuggled to India, Blake feared that his efforts to free them would become extremely difficult, if not impossible.

After referring to the railway timetable, Blake took a taxi to the Stephens' residence, carrying two small kitbags. He then visited Inspector Spur and requested the police to be on the qui vive. Finally, he alighted at the entrance to the West End hotel.

He allowed the hall porter to carry his bags inside. He wrote down his name as Mr Joseph Wry, travelling representative, in the hotel register. Blake was shown to his room where he had a much-needed bath. Refreshed, he was awaiting his tea, when he heard a slight rustle outside the door. A few minutes later, a waiter brought in a tea tray and set it down within easy reach. Blake made no move to drink his tea and continued reading the *Daily News*.

'Saheb, baper's shu jumso than shak, kabad ne kachubar ke?'

Blake reacted by sitting bolt upright on hearing these words, pretending to be pleasantly surprised.

'A jarthosti. Here! Ahiya kahathi futi mikalio?'

'I'm a student studying for a diploma in journalism. I have to work to make my way here.'

The Parsee, in the guise of a waiter, was hoping to catch Blake by surprise by speaking to him in Gujarati. He had asked in the vernacular if Blake would like to have a Parsee dish for lunch.

'Yes, by all means. To tell you the truth, I haven't tasted it for the last three months since I came to England,' Blake replied.

When the waiter left, Blake had to resist the temptation to follow him. He had to wait for Beram to make a move. After getting dressed, as Blake stepped out of his room, the door to the room opposite to his opened and a well-groomed man came out. He gave Blake a courteous bow, as fellow guests generally do in select hotels. Meeting the waiter in the passage, Blake told him he would be returning at 8.30 after taking a stroll in the park.

Blake deliberately left his room to give the Parsees the opportunity to examine his belongings if they knew where he was staying and to see if he was followed. When he returned from his walk, he noticed a taxi standing before the entrance steps and saw someone hurry down and enter the waiting car. Blake saw it was the man who had come out of the room opposite his.

'Rose Cottage, Queenly Street,' Blake heard the man say.

On hearing these words, Blake started, remembering

that the tramp on Martin's street had remembered hearing the word 'rose'. But Blake sensed that the man had wanted him to overhear the address. It sounded like the proverbial invitation from the spider to the fly.

Chapter XXIX

'He's arrived,' announced one of the servants set to keep watch.

The man they were expecting was like a thorn in their path, and what was worse, he belonged to their own community.

'At last. You know what to do,' said Beram. 'Rustom, you have to get away. One of us must remain free.'

'This is Rose Cottage, I believe?' Blake disguised as Aspandiar asked the servant who opened the door.

'Yes sir.'

'Is the master of the house in?'

'Yes sir, but he has given orders not to be disturbed.'

'Very well. It's very urgent business. If anything goes wrong, you will be the one blamed for it.'

'If you will step into the drawing room, I will take your card to him. If the boss cuts up rough, sir, it will be up to you to speak for me.'

'Quite,' said Blake

When he was seated in the luxuriously furnished hall, he handed the servant a card. He glanced about the room as if admiring its appointments while he noted the doors leading to other rooms. A baby grand piano was in one corner and a huge chandelier, decorated with artistic clusters of electric bulbs, hung in the centre of the ceiling. A chesterfield with armchairs placed all around formed a complete drawing room suite. In the corner opposite the piano there was a square table with a miniature replica of the Tower of Silence.

Five minutes later, Beram entered the room, stylishly dressed in a morning suit with a felt hat in his left hand, as if he were on his way out. The two men shook hands politely.

'Me' thariutuj ke' tame' more' v'eh'ell'e ahiya avso,' Beram spoke first, carefully watching the effect his words had on Blake. 'You may be surprised, but I was expecting you, Aspandiar.'

'Not at all,' Blake calmly replied. 'In fact, that's why I came here, my dear Beram.'

Beram's left eye contracted almost imperceptibly but Blake observed the tic.

'The more fool you, my friend. I suppose you expect to get out of here as easily as you came in.'

'Nothing easier, I promise you. God helps those who help themselves.'

'I admire the self-confidence you display. Never say die and all that. It's undoubtedly an excellent maxim to console those whose hopes are in vain.'

'On the contrary, I have never felt more confident that you will be unable to hold me against my will. I could leave this very minute, but that would hardly suit my purpose.' Blake leaned back in his chair, crossing his legs. 'You don't mind my smoking here, do you?'

'You will excuse me, but I can't bear tobacco smoke and what's more, smoking is not allowed in my house,' said Beram.

Blake immediately put his pipe and box of matches back into his coat pocket.

'Now then, fire away. Ask any questions you like. Whether you will be rewarded by answers is a different matter altogether.'

'Who are you?' Beram asked.

'Where is Blake?' countered Blake.

'Safe in India.'

'And Tinker.'

'You think I am fool enough to tell you everything? Although I am confident that you will never leave here, I will not be tempted to tell you how we did it.'

'But you are afraid,' Blake taunted. 'Of course, a gentleman who kidnaps a helpless child must needs be a brave man.'

'I don't believe the editor has the same intense feelings for his religion as we have for ours. It unfortunately became imperative to threaten him with his child. He may finally realize his mistake. Our religion is as sacred to us as his child is to him. And he did it all for filthy lucre, not caring a jot about the effect of such a sacrilegious act on the loyal hearts of Parsees, who are true to the British cause in India. If we kept our temples and Towers of Silence away from the gaze of durvands out of mere secretiveness, the actions of those marauding photographers would perhaps be justified. But we do so out of sheer necessity because it is one of the basic tenets of our religion.'

Blake's initial reaction when he heard about the Parsees' plans for vengeance had been to put it down to hollow sentiments and unreasoned fanaticism. But Beram's tone was so subtly persuasive and displayed such clear logic that it did not fail to impress him.

'This is a crime of individuals and not of Englishmen en masse. Hence it is our primary duty to teach them a severe lesson, howsoever cruel it may seem to others. It will also deter others from following suit. What grieves me most is to see you, a follower of our Lord, playing Judas!'

'Henceforth, you can consider me a non-Zoroastrian,' Blake said.

'Shame on you. You deserve to die. Since you care more for your English friends than your religion, it will be my special endeavour to make you a witness to their sufferings before I turn to you. You may as well know that you will soon join your friends on my yacht *Mineros* and will be sent on a voyage to India.'

Hearing this, Blake sprang to his feet and leapt in the air, grabbing the huge chandelier as the trapdoor beneath his chair opened and swallowed the chair. With the impetus of the upward leap, he swung high. With one hand, he pulled out something from his waist belt and used it to whip the six men who came running to Beram's assistance. Then, in a breathtaking acrobatic feat, Blake released hold of the chandelier, thinking he would land on Beram's shoulders.

But instead, he landed on bare ground and was

instantly enveloped in dense smoke. When the smoke thinned, Blake saw before him six prone forms, but Beram had disappeared. He then gave a shrill whistle and Pedro bounded in, followed by the chauffeur, who was none other than Inspector Spur and several plainclothes men, who spread out to search the premises.

Behind Beram's chair, a door stood ajar. Blake dashed through in to a very narrow passage. He had taken a few steps when something dark and as big as a cricket ball shot from one side of the wall. It missed his head by a fraction of an inch.

From the light of his torch, Blake saw it was one of a deadly species of Indian spider covered with a thick growth of long hair. It possessed a capacity to spring at its prey from a distance of two yards with the swiftness of an arrow. Its normal prey was birds and small reptiles, but it was fearless and not afraid to attack animals or even men. Blake drew out his revolver and, with a warning to Pedro to stand back, he shot the spider dead.

On hearing the shot, two policemen arrived. While one stopped to make sure Blake and Pedro were unharmed, the other continued down the passageway. He had hardly taken half a dozen steps, when Blake saw him disappear. Steadying himself, Blake took a step forward, and leaned over the brink of the opening, his revolver at the ready.

'Are you all right?' he shouted to the policeman who appeared to have fallen through a trap door.

'Yes,' came a faint reply. 'It's a well, and the water is deep enough for me to swim in.'

'Hang in there. Help is on the way.'

Leaving the rescue to others, Blake returned to the hall to question the prisoners who had now come to. But Inspector Spur informed him that the captives were just riffraff hired off the street. Blake was left with only the one new piece of information: that Tinker and the others were to be removed to India in Beram's yacht.

CHAPTER XXX

Blake was seated in an armchair, deeply engrossed in his own thoughts. He sat thus for the greater part of half an hour when the sound of the telephone bell roused him.

'Hello. This is Sir Henry speaking, Mr Blake.'

'But how in the name of...' began Blake, genuinely surprised that his whereabouts were known.

'Keep your hat on, old man. I persuaded Fairfax to tell me how to get in touch with you.'

'Oh chuck it. Come to the point, will you,' Blake heard a gasp in response to his impertinence but he was cross with Fairfax, the Inspector General of Police, for divulging his whereabouts.

'Are you prepared to accept a commission that will add a small fortune to your bank account?'

'I would rather see you hang but go on.'

'It's from the Raja of Gharabgola. He wishes you to proceed at once to India on an urgent mission.'

'Wait a moment. Have you already acquainted him with my whereabouts?' Blake asked.

'No. Fairfax insisted that the information be withheld

until you gave permission. At the same time, he wanted you to know all about this business.'

'This is a trap, Sir Henry, and nothing more. I shall be much obliged if you inform the Raja that I have already left for India, but that my exact whereabouts are not known.'

'Very well, if that is what you want,' came the disappointed response.

'You can offer him the services of a secret service man instead, although I am sure they will be refused.'

'Right ho! Anything else I can do for you?'

'Yes. Do not divulge my whereabouts but tell anyone who will listen that I have been travelling in very strange circles in India. If you have anything urgent to communicate, don't phone me directly but inform Fairfax about it instead, will you.'

'Understood.'

Blake carefully jammed tobacco into the bowl of his pipe and lit it. He returned to his armchair and meditatively blew rings of smoke. Beram's yacht had not been located and there was no trace of him or his associates. But Stephens had received a message offering to substitute him for the child. Blake knew that if no new leads appeared before the mail ship *Ramzak* left for India in three days time, he would have to allow the editor of *The Graphic* to sail on it because Stephens was determined to do anything to save his child. An advertisement in the *Times of India* had already been printed, as directed by the kidnappers, and further instructions were awaited.

Once again, Blake was disturbed, this time by a knock at the door by the wireless operator.

'Any news?'

'Yes sir. I received a message from the naval base a moment ago. The yacht *Mineros* was anchored until yesterday at the Downs, but her present whereabouts are not known.'

Blake decided that Beram had either disguised the yacht and moved her position, or that he had ordered her to set sail for India.

A servant came in with a telegram. Blake was waiting for information about Young as he was the Parsees' chief target. He hastily opened it and discovered that an attempt had been made to force the womenfolk at Young's house to divulge his whereabouts, but it was happily frustrated. Soon after, a note was delivered to Blake from Young himself, who expressed a wish to see him urgently. To facilitate a meeting, he had sent a car with the bearer of the note.

Blake slipped into the waiting car and was whisked away. More than once, Blake looked behind to see if he was being shadowed. The car stopped at the edge of a footpath at the end of which was a building with a name plate that read 'Aviator's Club'. The door was open and he walked inside. Blake went straight to a table on the right side of the room where Young stood up to receive him.

'Welcome. You've read the papers, I presume. Thank god I am saved from the forced boredom you have imposed on me.'

Looking at the blank expression on Blake's face, he handed Blake a copy of the newspaper.

'Read that,' he said, and flung himself upon a chair.

It is proposed to give a prize of £10,000 for an around the world flight that breaks the existing record by ten days. The donor is an eastern potentate who wishes to remain anonymous. For terms and conditions, apply to the office of the *Daily Herald* before the 20th instant, on which date the entries will close.

The news item also contained a list of seven names of the committee, which included three American magnates, a cabinet minister and an influential native ruler in India, namely, the Raja of Gharabgola.

Blake realized this was a bold attempt by Beram to get at Young. All he would need to do would be to wait for Young to land in Calcutta, a necessary stop if he participated in the contest. He knew it would be as difficult to prevent Young from entering the competition as it was to prevent Stephens from doing what he could to rescue his child. Blake would have to watch over both men.

'With the experience I have of the East, I stand a good chance of bagging the prize, don't you think?'

'Are you bent upon it?' Blake asked.

'Yes, of course I am,' Young replied.

'Alright then. Draw your chair near and listen carefully. If, after hearing what I have to say, you still persist, it's your business. By the way, what is the previous record?'

'Thirty-eight days.'

CHAPTER XXXI

In the gay and cosmopolitan city of Bombay, a taxi drove up to the gates of the office of the Commissioner of Police, opposite Crawford Market.

The taxi driver got down and entered the compound. At the head of the staircase, he went straight to the end of the passage, passing other departments. At the office of Commissioner Melley, he handed a card to one of the two peons who were stationed outside.

'Give this to the sahib,' the driver said in Hindi.

When the peon hesitated, the driver warned him that a personal friend of Mr Melley was impatiently waiting in his car, and that if he did not hurry he would find himself in a fine pickle.

At this, the man tightened his dhoti under his long coat, adjusted his pagree, and entered Mr Melley's office. He handed the commissioner the driver's card. Mr Melley looked at it as if he could scarcely believe his eyes. He then thrust it into his assistant's hands, who, in turn, looked no less perturbed. As the commissioner nodded to the peon to show the visitor in, his assistant got up and withdrew to an invisible recess from where he could watch without being seen.

'If it were not for my influence, my friend, it would have taken at least six months before you got to see the commissioner. You must understand, I have done all this for you, although you are a stranger, in no expectation of anything. Now hurry up and fetch your master from the car.'

In reply, the driver shoved the startled peon aside and entered the room himself.

The peons were grievously disappointed that the worm had not only forgotten to compensate them for their role in paving his way inside the commissioner's office, but had treated their authority with contempt. Of course, if it had been a white man in place of a lowly Hindu, things might have been easier to bear. But for one of their own sect to treat them thus! Better a kick from a European than such contempt from an Indian, that too a taxi driver.

'Good morning Melley, hope you recognize me!' the taxi driver said in an accent that contrasted sharply with his outward appearance.

'Mr Blake, the disguise is perfect and I must admit, you have mastered the lingo to a T!'

'You must be anxious to know the reason for my visit,' Blake began. 'Will you allow me to visit Young in his prison cell?'

'There is no hope for him, Mr Blake. He has committed a most dastardly murder and the proof is conclusive. What is your interest in him and who has commissioned you on his behalf?'

'As you know, Young was on a flight around the world, intending to break the former record and thus bag the £10,000 prize. He knew his name would appear in the papers as one of the contestants. He has bitter enemies here in India and was afraid an attempt would be made on his life when he landed here. So he engaged my services to safeguard himself against all eventualities. I was tempted because it offered a novel experience and I consented to be his companion on the plane.

'After we landed in Calcutta, we railed down to Bombay to fulfil one of the conditions of the contest, namely to report personally to either the Raja or the Kumar of Gharabgola at the Taj Mahal Hotel. We arrived at Victoria Terminus and were taken to the Taj. We met the Kumar and he congratulated us for being the first to arrive at Calcutta. After the meeting, we were asked to attend the reception in our honour later that night and then we returned to out double suite.

'At the scheduled time, Young presented himself alone. As planned, our host was told I was in bed with a severe headache. This allowed me to keep a watch on Young, while a hireling took my place in bed with a bandage tied round his head. Dancing was still in progress at two in the morning. I had kept Young in my sights all evening but turned to pick up a cup of coffee placed on the counter. In that brief space of time, I lost sight of him.

'I checked our suite but he was not there. I returned

to the ballroom and tried to scrutinize each and every face. I had to be careful and it is due to this caution that I am here to tell the tale. When I couldn't find him in the ballroom, I went to the terrace.

'From there I went back to our apartment, where I found my substitute securely gagged and tied. After loosening his cords, I asked him to remain in place until a search was made for Young, upon whose finding he would be set free. Because of the treatment that my substitute had received, I was convinced that Young had met foul play. Back in the ballroom I noticed a slight commotion. The crowd had noticed Young's absence. Servants were sent to our room, but they only found the man left on my bed. There was no trace of Young and no word about him until I read about his being arrested for murder this morning. I would be grateful, Melley, if you can tell me about the circumstances of his arrest and allow me to interview him.'

Before Melley has been appointed commissioner, Blake and he had been great friends. The detective had also helped Commissioner Melley solve a riddle of a private nature, so he did not hesitate. He picked up a cigar box and held it open to Blake. After taking a cigar for himself, he lit it and then leaned forward to look Blake in the eye.

'Do you believe in your heart of hearts that Young is innocent?'

'Yes, I am absolutely sure he is innocent,' Blake replied.

'Perhaps your opinion will change when you have

heard the facts. Several people present remember seeing Young at 2 a.m. last night. The man who was murdered less than a hundred yards away from the hotel had a watch that appears to have stopped working at 2.05 when its dial was broken by a knife thrust. The fingers of the victim were tightly clutching a torn collar, showing that a struggle had taken place between the assailant and the victim. Whilst searching the grounds, this cufflink was found.'

Melley paused to take out a pocket book from a drawer in his desk and laid it before Blake for inspection.

'Do you recognize it?'

'Yes. It belongs to Young.'

'We used our specially trained bloodhound to trace him. After sniffing at the ripped collar, the dog immediately caught the scent and led the police straight to Young. He was lying across the Cooperage railway crossing tracks with his neck on a rail, apparently planning to commit suicide. As soon as he saw the police, he sprang up and attempted to run away. When he was brought to the police station, his clothes were stained with blood. The cufflink on his shirtsleeve matched the one found on the grounds.'

Blake sat aghast. But even now, when hope seemed bleak, he managed to not lose heart and continued to maintain full faith in Young. He was convinced that this was a plot engineered by Beram to punish the aviator for his foolishness. But he found it hard to believe that Beram would bring himself to commit murder and then throw the blame on another. Still, facts were facts and

Blake could scarcely go against them. It was possible that Young had killed the man in self-defence and then lost his head and tried to commit suicide. He was sure an interview with the prisoner would clear things up.

'Was the collar lying on top of the murdered man's hand?'

'On the contrary, it was so tightly clenched that it could not be removed without breaking open the stiffened fingers.'

'When did the police hear about the murder?'

'At four in the morning.'

'At what time was Young arrested?'

'At 5 a.m.'

'Where was the wound inflicted on the victim?'

'There was a big gash on his throat.'

'Do you know the name of the murdered man?'

'No, there was not a single trace found on him to prove his identity.'

'To what community did the dead man belong?'

'From the sudreh and kusti found on his person, it would appear he was a Parsee. Things are looking black for your friend,' Melley said sympathetically. 'I myself feel sorry for him. Unfortunately, he refused to admit to where he has thrown or hidden the victim's belongings. The Parsees will wax furious at this. Without knowing the name of the deceased, the death ceremonies cannot proceed and the body will not be allowed into the regular Tower of Silence. They will utilize all their resources to see that Young suffers the full penalty under the law. This incident will reopen an old wound, namely the photo of

the Tower of Silence that was published in *The Graphic*.
And in such troubled times of Gandhi's non-cooperation
movement, we are in need of the sympathy and staunch
support of this small but influential community.'

Saying this, he pressed an electric button on his desk.
The mighty peon of our acquaintance entered in answer
to the summons and was shocked to see the taxi driver
seated in a place of honour, conferring with his sahib,
while better men (in his opinion) were rarely allowed
more than a five-minute interview.

'Herbert saab ko bulao,' ordered Melley. 'Herbert
will take you to the inspector in charge at the Esplanade
police station. Here's a letter of introduction and this
badge will ensure you get past the police force herd.'

Mr Herbert came in and Melley instructed him to
introduce Blake to Inspector Sharp at the Esplanade
police station. Once outside, Blake was careful to maintain
his disguise by addressing Herbert in the vernacular and
following respectfully a little distance behind. He also
ran forward to open the door for Herbert before taking
his seat at the wheel.

CHAPTER XXXII

At the Esplanade police station, there were specially built cells to keep prisoners for up to two remands of a fortnight each. There were two classes of cells: one for Europeans and another for Indians.

In one of the European cells, a dejected Young was sitting on the one-foot high plank that also served as a bed. He was so lost in thought that he did not look up even when the big padlock was removed with a rattle and Blake was ushered in. It was only when Blake laid his hand upon Young's shoulders that he looked up with a start. When he recognized his visitor, he sprang up with a cry of joy and hope.

'Blake!' he said, and then broke down sobbing.

'Keep heart, old man. I won't leave a stone unturned to get you out of here.'

'What am I supposed to have done?'

The tone of his query convinced Blake that Young was innocent. He was now sure this was a trap set by his astute enemies.

'The long and short of it is that they accuse you of

killing a man last night. The circumstantial evidence against you is quite strong.'

'What? A murder?'

'For my part, I am convinced you are innocent.'

'God bless you for your faith in me, Blake. I wouldn't willingly harm a fly, much less murder a human being in cold blood.'

Sitting beside him on the wooden plank, Blake related all the facts he had gathered from Commissioner Melley. Young grew pale as he listened to Blake, looking like someone who had received a severe whack to the head with a heavy blunderbuss.

'Try to calm yourself and tell me where you went last night and why you left the ballroom'.

'That's simple. I met a beautiful young lady, who was an acquaintance of mine before I left India. While dancing with her, an uncontrollable desire overtook me to accompany her home.'

'Was it at her suggestion?' interrupted Blake.

'Yes, coming to think of it. It was she who suggested it. But in the name of goodness, you don't mean to suggest...' and here Young stopped in mute consternation.

'I don't believe she was consciously involved, but I am afraid she was an innocent tool in unscrupulous hands.'

'But...'

'Wait, let me finish. As I warned you, you have been targeted. Beram and his lot have gone to great lengths to achieve their goal. It is not unlikely that they will have made themselves fully acquainted with your life in India, your friends, especially ones like Mademoiselle—' here he looked questioningly at Young.

'Miss Mary Herbert,' obliged the latter.

'Well then! Knowing of your warm friendship with Ms Herbert, they could presume you would try to meet her at your first opportunity!'

'But then I don't understand how—'

'It's useless to guess at this stage. I don't know what trick they resorted to but I will find out when I see her. Do you remember her address?' Blake asked, pad and pencil in hand.

'She lives with her widowed mother at Colaba Chambers.'

'Now, tell me how you escaped without my seeing you leave.'

'I felt it a unique challenge to outwit you,' and here Young almost smiled. 'It wasn't easy. Whenever I looked in your direction, your eyes were on me. The chance came when you turned around to order a cup of tea or coffee. Ms Herbert and I slipped into the lift, which is adjacent to the ballroom. Working the lift myself, we went down and then out into the night. We footed it to her place, walking hand in hand.

'She opened the front door with her latch key and we went inside. Her mother was asleep. So was the servant, but she was roused from her sleep and served us a meal of cold fowl and chickpeas, and a bottle or two of wine. Then she left us alone. We did justice to the food and drank freely of the wine. Before we knew it, two hours had flown by.

'I left her at about 4.30 in the morning, walking to the hotel on somewhat unsteady legs. I had hardly gone twenty yards when I saw a taxi crawling at a snail's pace towards me. I hailed it and told the driver to take me to the hotel. I don't remember what happened after that, except for a hazy recollection of a railway crossing.'

'Had you a watch on you?'

'Yes, a gold one.'

'You cannot account for the blood stains on your clothes?'

'No.'

'Perhaps you or she might have cut a finger? Try to remember whether any bottles were broken or a glass.'

'Nothing was broken.'

Blake had now to put his theory to the test. There was no time to waste in view of the fact that Young would be brought before the magistrate at noon. If he wished to have any results that would be helpful in Young's case, he had to act before the inquest was held.

'I must put my theory to test, old chap. Time is running out. I need to complete my investigation before the inquest is held. Try to keep your spirits up.'

After warmly shaking hands with the prisoner, Blake went straight from the cell to see Inspector Sharp.

'You took a jolly long time,' remarked that worthy. Sharp had already convinced himself of Young's guilt, and believed all Blake's efforts a waste of time.

Blake ignored the comment and asked to inspect Young's blood-stained clothing.

'Of course. At once,' he replied.

'There is no government laboratory close by, is there?' Blake asked after examining the stains on Young's clothing with a magnifying glass.

'No, the nearest is ten miles away at Parel.'

'Would you mind sending this jacket to the laboratory immediately to test the stains? If you need to get the sanction of a higher authority, I can ...'

'That's all right Mr Blake. Is there anything else I can do for you?'

'Yes. Please accompany me to the morgue so I can examine the victim's body in your presence.'

In the morgue, the sheet covering the body was removed. Before beginning his examination, Blake stood for a few moments viewing it from a distance.

'Humm,' he grunted.

Blake had a lot of experience and knowledge with the bodies of murder victims and others who had come to an untimely end. After his examination, although he was sure that his conclusions were correct, he requested that the inspector send for two eminent medical practitioners to corroborate his views.

'I will pay their fees myself,' Blake said, with a view to overcoming any hesitation on the part of Inspector Sharp.

While he waited, he bent down and examined the wound on the murdered man's throat with the aid of his magnifying glass. He then took out his notebook and scribbled a note to the commissioner and directed it to be sent to him immediately.

Dear Melley – Would you please have inquiries made at all the hospitals in Bombay, as well as in all private surgical practices, to ask if any patient has succumbed after surgery for a throat tumour in the past ten hours. Very truly yours, Blake.

Blake then examined the collar that had been tightly clutched in the dead man's fingers.

'Found anything yet?' Sharp asked sarcastically.

'Not of much count,' Blake replied evasively.

He then removed a small packet from his notebook and pulled out a pinch of powder which he proceeded to sprinkle on a smudge at the centre of the collar. After some manipulations, a clear thumb mark appeared on the white surface. Pointing to it, he asked the inspector to have photographs taken and requested a copy for himself. Next, Blake's curiosity was aroused by the curious way the bootlaces were tied on the dead man's feet. To satisfy himself, he unlaced the boot on the right foot. After removing it, he examined the sole of the foot, noting a thin metal ring nearly buried into the flesh of the big toe. Blake replaced the boot, leaving the laces undone, while the inspector watched, looking bored.

Doctors Portern and Bharacha entered the room together. One was an Englishman, and the other a Parsee, both M.D.s and eminent specialists. After being introduced, Blake requested that they examine the body to determine when the man had died.

After a thorough examination, they left the room with Blake and gave him their considered opinion. Blake returned and asked where the murdered man's telltale watch was, knowing it was the most dangerous piece of evidence against Young. Blake then took his leave of the inspector, saying they would meet again later at the Chief Presidency Magistrate's court.

On his way to the commissioner's office, Blake stopped at Victoria Terminus to use a public telephone box.

'Hello! Is that the Parel Laboratory? I'm from the commissioner's office. Have you received a blood stained jacket for analysis?'

'Yes, we received it a few minutes ago.'

'When will your report be ready?'

'By 9 a.m. tomorrow, at the latest.'

Blake hung up and returned to his taxi, driving towards Crawford Market. Outside the commissioner's office, he pushed the peon unceremoniously aside and entered unannounced. The commissioner was not alone. Blake immediately recognized the young lady from Young's description as Miss Herbert.

'Hello. The very man I wished to see. Come and join us and see if you can make anything out of what this charming young lady says.'

'Will you kindly once again relate your story for my friend…' began Melley but Blake interrupted him by raising his hand.

'Is it true, Ms Herbert, that Young left you at quarter to five this morning?' Blake asked.

'Yes.'

'And at what time did you both leave the hotel?'

'At about two in the morning.'

The Tower of Silence -5 165

'You walked straight to your place, I suppose?'

'Yes.'

'Was your mother sleeping when you entered?'

Ms Herbert could only nod at him in dumb surprise.

'What do you do for a living?'

'I am a teacher in the Cathedral Girls' High School.'

'What is the salary you are paid?'

'Really, sir,' she protested, turning to Melley, with flushed cheeks, 'I don't understand how it concerns...'

The commissioner was a bit nonplussed but after a glance at Blake, he persuaded her to reply if she really wished to save the life of her friend.

'Three hundred rupees per month,' she said, her cheeks flushed a beetroot red. 'But I have private tuitions to call upon.'

'Have you had a new pupil within this fortnight?'

'Yes, my services were engaged only three days ago by a Parsee gentleman, to coach his daughter.'

'In spite of paying you handsomely, she comes to your place, is it not? Tell me, did you know that Young would be at the Taj hotel last night?'

'Yes, but quite by chance. The day before the ball, my new pupil informed me she was going with her father to the Taj in honour of Young, who was the first to reach Bombay in the flight around the world competition. She asked if I would like to accompany her there. I welcomed the opportunity to meet Mr Young again after so long.'

'But what made you ask Young to accompany you to your place at so late an hour?'

'I thought myself unusually clever, that's all.'

'Please explain, and be as brief as you can,' Blake said tartly, making her winch at the discourtesy.

'An hour before the ball, I received a note stating that if I wished to save Young's life, I had better entice him to my place at 2.00 a.m., and employ all my arts to keep him there.'

CHAPTER XXXIII

The Gujarati papers were full of news of the murder perpetrated by an Englishman. A Parsee had not only been murdered in cold blood, but all traces of his identity had been removed, thus preventing his body from being honourably disposed of at the Tower of Silence. There seemed no possibility of putting the body to rest before sunset, even after the inquest was done.

At noon, the prisoner was to be put on remand before the Chief Presidency Magistrate in the Esplanade Police Court. Knowing that the tempers of the Parsees were inflamed and fearing that perhaps the prisoner might be handled roughly by the mob, the police made arrangements to stand the prisoner in the magistrate's private chamber, instead of in the courtroom.

The disappointed crowd dispersed, but found a rallying point at the place where an inquest was shortly to be held by the coroner at 2 p.m. Ten minutes before the scheduled time, the sergeant was asked to choose seven persons from the crowd to form a jury for the inquest. With the formalities settled, the inquiry began. The Raja of Gharabgola was the first witness to be examined.

'Will you kindly relate all you know about the incident?' the coroner asked.

'There is nothing much to tell, as far as I am concerned,' replied the Raja nervously. 'I gave a ball in honour of Mr Young at the Taj Mahal Hotel. All went swimmingly, until he was found unaccountably missing at around 2.30 in the morning. We dispersed after that.'

Ten other persons were examined, all verifying that Young was missing from the party just after two. To connect the time link between the disappearance of Young from the Taj and the murdered man, the latter's broken watch was produced.

'A slit on the murdered man's shirt proves that Young first tried to stab him in the heart. The victim tried to ward off the blow and the knife struck the dial of the watch, stopping it at 2.05 a.m.' Inspector Sharp was giving his testimony. 'After the first unsuccessful attack, Young then struck at the man's throat and killed him. But the victim must have struggled as evidenced by the piece of Young's collar clenched in his hand. There was also a cufflink found near the dead man, proving Young was in the vicinity because the other link was found on a sleeve of his blood-stained shirt when he was arrested.'

An angry murmur went through the crowded hall. The last witness testified that he had seen the suspect with a torn shirt and an expression of horror on his face, running away like a frightened cur close to the Taj.

'Did you mark the time?' asked the coroner.

'No,' came the reply, in almost hesitating tones that

gave a veneer of honesty to his testimony. 'I do however remember that it was shortly after the clock in my house chimed two o'clock.'

'Have you any questions for this witness, gentleman?' the coroner asked the jury. There was silence for a time, but then one of the jurors raised his hand.

'What were you doing there at that time of the night?' the juror asked.

The witness seemed taken aback at first but then recovered his composure.

'I suffer from insomnia. I walked out for some fresh air to escape the stifling atmosphere of my bedroom.'

'How long have you resided at your place?' the juror persisted.

The question was met with unrest and impatience from the audience, prompting the coroner to warn the crowd that he would clear the room if the noise continued.

'I arrived from Bangalore on the evening of the previous day. I was staying at my friend's place before proceeding to Po–, er, I mean Surat, tomorrow.'

The coroner then inquired if anybody with knowledge of the events wished to speak. The audience, who were mainly Parsees, looked around as if daring anyone to speak in defense of a man they would rather have seen given summary justice.

Suddenly, there was commotion near the entrance. Someone was trying to force his way in, not caring a jot who he pushed out of the way. Matters were beginning to take a serious turn, when the police happily intervened, and a path was formed for the intruder to enter. The whole congregation murmured in surprise when they saw a respectable looking middle-aged Parsee gentlemen with a pagree on his head, closely followed by a beautiful young Englishwoman and a sergeant carrying a bundle in his hands.

'What is the meaning of this?' thundered the coroner in as haughty a tone as he could command.

The intruder raised his hands to command silence and be heard. The gesture, as well as something in his bearing that savoured of authority and strength, had the desired effect.

'Sir and gentlemen of the jury, I have information to impart regarding this unfortunate tragedy. Have I your permission to speak?'

On seeing the coroner nod, he continued.

'Miss Mary Herbert, will you please inform the court what you know of the matter?'

All necks craned forward for a glimpse of the beautiful young woman. The crowd listened in silence as she unfolded the events of the case. When she was done, someone in the crowd shouted that it was all a put up affair to shield the culprit, while others shouted, 'Proof! Proof!' and still others called out, 'Quiet! Quiet!'

'Can you corroborate your version with proof, Miss Herbert?' the coroner asked.

'Eh-be-latoo bani geyoch,' came a voice from the audience. Like a sensible man, the coroner ignored the man.

'Yes, sir,' the Parsee who had led her in spoke up,

quieting the crowd who were eager to hear what one of their own had to say.

'Let me first of all introduce myself. I am one of the factors of Messrs Borrow and Right, the well-known firm of private detectives and inquiry agents. Being on the spot here in Bombay and present on the night in question at the Taj Mahal Hotel, I set an inquiry afoot from the very minute Mr Young disappeared from the hotel. At first I thought it was Mr Young himself who had met with foul play, but this suspicion was removed on reading the morning papers. You will no doubt judge for yourselves about his guilt or innocence after I tell you what my investigations revealed.'

Taking the bundle from the sergeant, he slowly opened it. Having prepared himself as a conjurer does, he addressed the court.

'You will be surprised to learn that the murdered man is not a Parsee and I have ample evidence to prove it. I request the court and the jury to approach the body of the dead man, in the interests of justice, and make a careful observation of what I am going to point out.'

At this they all adjourned to the where the body was kept. After it was uncovered, the man they took for a Parsee lifted up the shirt of the dead person, till the kusti was visible to all.

'Note that the sudreh is not worn on the right side, but upside down. Further, the kusti is also not tied in the orthodox style. There are inexplicable mistakes in tying the knots.'

The Parsee jury members and some priests and

scholars present all leaned closer to examine each item. A look of trepidation passed through the observers like a wave. But the coroner and non-Parsee members of the jury seemed unconvinced. At this, the man yanked off the boot from the right leg of the murder victim.

'Look first at the toe. Is it not self-explanatory?' he asked, turning towards a Hindu jury member. 'The ring on the toe is conclusive proof that the dead man is not a Parsee, but a Hindu. What is more, the ring has been worn so long on that toe it has well-nigh eaten into the flesh. But, for the clinching evidence, observe the state of the sole of his foot. Does it belong to a man who is used to wearing boots? Now look at the knots in the laces of the boot on the left leg. The evidence suggests the man was not in the habit of tying kusti knots. Lastly, look at the wound on his throat before we return to the hall.'

Once back in the hall, the man handed the coroner a paper before starting to speak. 'That paper, sir, is a certificate from Dr Demontie. It states that the dead man was operated upon in a poor neighbourhood for a throat tumour but died two hours after the surgery. As he was a penniless mendicant, his body was sent to the Government Medical College for dissection for the sake of science. But instead of it being sent to the hospital, the corpse was dressed up like a Parsee and left on the roadside, for purposes best known to some person or persons unknown.'

The excitement in the room was unprecedented. The foremost emotion was fury at the thought that someone might have attempted to pollute their dokhma. At the very same moment, the man speaking on Young's behalf detected a faint odour of a pleasant oriental scent. He knew from whom the pleasant smell emitted, but made no sign to reveal his observation.

'Gentlemen, do you think that Mr Young could have performed the miracle of dressing the man up between 2 a.m. when he came out of the hotel, and 2.05 when the murder was committed, as instanced by the dead man's watch?'

'No, no, no,' shouted the crowd, now enthusiastically in favour of the very man whom they had been prepared to kill but half an hour ago.

'Over and above this, gentlemen, the collar clenched by the hand of the dead man, as well as the blood-stained shirt found on the person of Mr Young, and which is now in the possession of the police, both still have the back collar button. The real culprits stole a shirt from the wardrobe of Mr Young while he was at Miss Herbert's place, and put it in the clutches of the dead man. It is also how the bloodhound was able to pick up Mr Young's scent because the collar was from one of his own shirts.

'Gentlemen, considering the evidence put before us, I am convinced that the man died following an operation and from no other cause. I am also convinced Mr Young had nothing to do with it. Those who agree kindly raise your hands.'

Chapter XXXIV

Let us devote this chapter to some clarifications. What seemed clear at the inquest was nowhere near as straightforward to piece together. It was full of plots and counterplots and ingenious contrivances, befitting the two gigantic intellects involved. For instance, let us hasten to remove the illusion from the minds of our readers that the detective who so ably fought on Young's behalf at the inquest was Blake himself.

Blake had done the needful by ferreting out the true state of affairs. What the astute criminologist was worried about was Beram's next move after the inquest. Taking Melley alone into his confidence, Blake decided it was prudent to protect Young. Blake also asked an agent to attend the inquest and to be on the lookout for that rare oriental scent to which Beram was partial.

Meanwhile, Beram was striding up and down in an office situated on the fourth floor of a palatial building on Hornby Road. There remained only nine days for the anniversary of the cursed day the photo was taken of the Tower of Silence.

'Strange, strange, this premonition. I almost feel his

eyes are upon me.' Beram thought to himself. 'If the advocate at the inquest hall was Blake in disguise, he would have noticed the special scent and would not have failed to shadow me or deputed someone else to do so. Perhaps it was not Blake in disguise. But by now, Rustom would have spirited Young away from his cell. With Young safely away, and the three others picked up from Europe, even if Blake does raid our hiding place, our mission will have well-nigh ended.'

Chapter XXXV

Bump! Somebody had apparently bumped hard against the door behind which Tinker, the Baron and Martin were imprisoned.

Their prison was a comfortably furnished, big, square room. The surface of the walls was as smooth as glass. The skylight in the roof, which was the only source of light and air, was thirty feet above the floor. The trio had made several futile attempts to scale the walls to reach the skylight, even forming a human ladder, but Tinker's fingers were a full seven feet away from the top.

Meals were supplied to them regularly and twice a day each prisoner was taken out under the escort of two very swarthy personalities to an adjacent room to satisfy their natural needs, and perform their morning and evening ablutions. On the eighteenth day of their imprisonment, they were awakened out of their lethargy by the loud bump. Then, the door was thrown open and three men came in, almost at once. The door slammed shut behind them, though not before a rat contrived to slip in undetected. The new entrants were none other than Stephens, Young and Beram.

'Stephens! By god! So they have succeeded in bagging you too,' Tinker cried.

'And Young! They got you,' the Baron sobbed.

'Stephens is here of his own free will as a substitute for his child. Mr Young, this is Tinker. You know him by reputation, I believe.' Beram said coolly. 'My dear Baron, I sincerely trust you have not forgotten our friendship at the hotel in misty London. Don't hold it against me. Business is business, you know, as the sordid old Scot said to his dirty Irish mates. Mr Young, let me assure you, is also here of his own accord. And Martin, my fine fellow, you now have the opportunity to see how it feels to be a captive.'

Just then the six men noticed the rat and its scurrying attempts to find a way out along the four walls. It squeaked in fright as if it knew it was a death trap because there was not a crevice large enough for a fly to creep into at the joint between the smooth floor and the gleaming walls.

'I for the life of me can't guess who is the most unfortunate. The rat or you lot.'

'Oh, stop crowing. If we had been on equal terms, I would soon show you the error of your ways,' Tinker said boldly.

'Why, you will notice the odds are against me,' Beram retorted. 'The odds are five to one in your favour. My retreat is cut off, and I give you my word, my followers will not interfere. Sooner or later, you will all become prey to vultures so you may as well take this opportunity to do me in when I am totally at your mercy.'

'Why then, put up your dukes, you miserable rat of a Parsee crow,' Tinker said, removing his jacket and turning up his shirtsleeves, and preparing to rush upon his adversary.

'Stop,' Beram commanded in an authoritative voice.

To the surprise of all, the lad stopped dead in his tracks.

'I could have killed you for that filthy abuse. I will not retaliate in kind and stoop to your common level,' Beram said with a scornful look.

'Allow me to say a word,' Stephens intervened.

'My friend, I know what you are going to say. I will make allowances for the age of the uncouth lad and leave the fault of his behaviour to his ill breeding.'

Tinker's cheeks flushed scarlet at this. With the anger caused by Tinker's unguarded words still rankling in his mind, Beram's attention was diverted by the miserable activities of the rat. He reached out his hand in the direction of the frightened rodent, looked straight into its eyes, and pointed with the forefinger of his right hand to a spot in the centre of the floor. The rat obediently crept there and stayed quite still, as if it were dead. Then Beram beckoned to the Baron and Martin. The three men left the room, leaving Tinker with Stephens and Young.

'Two days more for the anniversary. That will be the beginning of the end,' the three men heard Beram say as he walked out.

CHAPTER XXXVI

With Beram gone, the three men began to exchange information before their host could come by and separate them again. But Stephens pulled them up short.

'Hang on, youngster. We can be observed from the skylight and overheard through the door. Let's be careful.' Then lowering his voice to a whisper, he continued. 'Blake gave me something for you that I have concealed in my left boot heel but I don't want to draw attention to it.'

'After a few minutes, you and Young should start complaining about your feet being sore from keeping your boots on for days. You can then remove them and put them beside mine. I will manage the rest.' Tinker suggested.

Stephens then related the whole turn of events which had led him into Beram's den.

'He fooled you and the governor both. The child was never here and it was not brought aboard the yacht,' Tinker said as Stephens and Young listened incredulously. 'It's the truth. The governor once said to me that Beram is not a cad, either by nature or education. The child was given to the charge of a very respectable home, and now that you are here, he must have been returned to his mother's charge and care'.

'Thank heavens. Poor Mary! Now she will be worrying about me and crying her heart out for allowing me to walk into this danger with open eyes.'

'Do you think Beram means half of what he says, Tinker?' Young asked.

'About what?'

'The vultures, of course.'

'I should think so. The governor did say once by way of warning that the Parsees are religious fanatics and once their religious sentiments are hurt, there is no one more dangerous.' Tinker replied.

It was then Young's turn to tell his tale.

'I was lying face down when my cell door opened. The Parsee superintendent ordered me to stand up. He then beckoned to someone standing outside and quietly left the room. The other chap hurriedly came in and bluntly asked me to choose between immediate escape or certain death, telling me the jury had decided against me. We exchanged clothes. I was given instructions about how to get out while he took my place in the cell.'

'But how would my master be able to keep you in sight?'

'Blake had soaked the soles of my boots with creosote, so that the scent of the oil could easily be tracked by a hound.'

'But it's been days since you left the prison, and the scent…'

'The scent of creosote remains fresh for several days, even when wet. I was taken from house to house until I was brought here through secret tunnels. I am expecting Blake to track me down. But if he doesn't and you manage to escape, Tinker, he has asked you to go to...' here Young bent down and whispered very softly in Tinker's ear.

'By Jove, Tinker, would you believe I haven't had my boots off for almost a week?' Young said in ordinary tones. He was shrewd enough not to talk too loudly and alert their captors to the trick.

'Same with me, old chap,' chimed in Stephens.

Removing their boots, they carelessly chucked them near where Tinker had suggested. They then resumed their discussion of Beram.

'Nothing is impossible with such an unscrupulous person, one who would not even stop at murder,' Stephens said.

'Who has he killed?'

'Why Maneyrol, of course. If he could control a rat by will, what could have stopped him from hypnotizing the Frenchman?'

Chapter XXXVII

That same night, Tinker stealthily got out of his bed in the pitch-dark room. A faint glimmer shone from the skylight of their prison chamber. He crept towards the door and listened intently. He heard faint but regular breathing, as if someone was asleep outside the door.

Tinker now stepped softly towards the wall opposite the door and began digging by means of the small but sharp instrument that had been hidden in the heel of Stephens's left boot. He worked patiently for an hour, and stopped only when he made an opening the size of a mouse hole. Into this hole he inserted a small piece of dynamite, tying one end of the wire to the bed and fixing the other to a fuse.

While Tinker was thus engaged, Young and Stephens were engaged in slowly tearing the bed sheet in half. When they were done, they knotted the ends together and tied one end with a wire that was then attached to a steel hook from the bed. Stephens and Young set the marble table against the wall. Stephens climbed on to it and stood with his hands resting against the wall. Young climbed onto his shoulders. Then it was Tinker's turn.

He climbed up with the hooked end of the sheet held firmly between his teeth.

Tinker, who was now standing upon Young's shoulders, steadied himself and then waved the bed sheet with the hook at the end and dexterously threw it against the horizontal iron bars of the skylight.

It was a chance they had to take to set themselves free. It was not a simple task, considering the darkness below and faint light above. If Tinker missed his aim, the momentum of the swing to the floor would carry him forward and he would certainly crash to the floor. But by one chance in a million, the hook caught the bar and Tinker gained support from the bed sheet that was now secured to the skylight. He swung himself up like a monkey. Holding the bar in one hand, he drew the other end of the sheet up and wound it around the bar securing it with a knot. The bedsheet now formed a swing where he could sit. Tinker took out a small file from his coat pocket and began filing through the bar.

In the meantime, Stephens and Young climbed down from the table and returned it to its former position. They lay down on the bed and looked up with amazement as Tinker performed his hazardous task. Within twenty minutes, he had filed through a bar. Bending one end outward, he quickly slipped out. Then he untied the knots and drew the sheet up. He untied the two cut pieces, tying one piece into a bundle while wrapping the other around himself as the Hindu women do with their sarees. He then disappeared from the view of his silent audience after a cheerful wave of his hand.

'Let's give him an hour before we try our luck?' whispered Young.

'To be on the safe side, let's try at 5 a.m.'

At 5 a.m., they pulled on their boots. Young untied the fuse from around the leg of the bed and carried the end to the opposite side of the wall, fixing it to the leg of a chair. After covering themselves with the bedding for protection, Young slipped his hand out and applied a match to the fuse. It burnt with lightning speed and reached its end in the hollow of the wall in the twinkling of an eye.

Bang! Crash! Thump! A great portion of the solid wall crumbled down, leaving a large opening below. No sooner did the two see the gap in the wall than they made a precipitous rush towards it.

Once outside, they found themselves in a garden.

'You take the straight road Stephens. I'll hide close by and take a chance with Beram's aeroplane if it is parked nearby,' Young said.

CHAPTER XXXVIII

Beram awoke from his sleep when he heard the deafening bang that shook the whole house.

Just as expected, he thought, not stirring from his bed. He heard the whole house bestir itself. People were running hither and thither. He heard a musical bell ring from the receiver attached to the bedpost.

'The prisoners have escaped. They blew open a hole in the wall.'

'Well?'

'I know we expected this but you did not think of everything. Jal who was keeping watch on the roof near the skylight was found but a minute ago, half smothered.'

Beram was pacing up and down like a panther. He knew that only Tinker could have managed the difficult job of escaping through the skylight. Blowing the wall was just to cover his flight. But what the other two do not realize, Beram thought with fiendish joy, is that I can summon Tinker here by sheer force of will.

Beram hurriedly performed his morning ablutions, dressed in nothing but a loincloth and a sudreh or mulmul shirt, and a velvet cap. After devoting ten minutes to reciting Hormuzd Khodae, he finished tying his kusti before changing his clothes. Ready for the day, Beram drew up a chair in the corner of his room and summoned Rustom.

'If Tinker returns, don't apprehend him. As for the others, take them to the places we discussed.'

After Rustom had bowed himself out, Beram began to recite sacred words and was instantaneously lost in deep concentration. He sat erect on the chair and seemed game to carry on for hours if need be, when Tinker entered the room. His movements were mechanical, like a somnambulist, and he stood before Beram as if awaiting orders. Only then did Beram wake from his trance. He first looked deep into Tinker's eyes and then ordered him to lie down on the bed. When Tinker was on his back, Beram bent over him.

'Go to sleep, my lad. And don't awake until I order you to do so,' Beram whispered gently, before he began to question him about his escape.

Tinker related everything that had transpired, including how he had overpowered Jal on the roof and his move to the railway station.

'Where did you go?'

'To Bombay. I got down at Victoria Terminus. I was just getting into a victoria when I heard your summons.'

'Where did you plan to go?'

'To see the police commissioner.'

'Why?'

At this point, Beram became concerned because Tinker seemed to have trouble breathing and his pulse was very weak. Afraid he might be permanently injured, Beram ordered him to wake up. It was fully five minutes before Tinker became fully conscious. When he looked around the room, he saw Beram sprawling on the chair beside him. He suddenly remembered feeling dizzy as he alighted at Victoria Terminus and his unaccountable return by the very next train to his starting point.

'Perhaps I am no longer hypnotized and under his influence,' thought Tinker.

But hearing Beram stir, he instantly pretended to still be under Beram's influence. Beram once again bent over Tinker, and examined his pulse and heart beat. Apparently satisfied, he began speaking in a monotonous voice.

'Go…to…sleep, go…to…sleep. There…there… you are go…ing into the land of dreams…you are fast asleep…fast…asleep…you cannot wake up…not until I order you to do so.'

Tinker gave a huge sigh and feigned unconsciousness.

'Tell me where Blake is.'

Tinker opened his mouth as if to say something, and then shut it, as if unwilling to give out the secret.

'Where is Blake?' Beram asked again.

'At Putao, in Burma.'

'What is he doing?'

'A tall dark man is whipping him mercilessly,' said Tinker, his face showing his discomfort. He tried to sit up arms outstretched before him, his eyes staring straight at Beram.

Beram's conscience was pricked on hearing this. What if Blake had been harmed in Putao despite the orders he had given that he be detained without suffering any privation or hardship? Beram once again engaged himself in awakening Tinker.

'You will implicitly obey me whenever I call you, wherever you may be. When you awake, you will forget everything.' Beram concluded.

'But I won't,' said a grim voice behind his back. 'Don't turn around. If you value your life, put your hands up. That's right. Now, right about turn. Good morning.

'Tinker, my boy, make him secure, will you.'

But Tinker continued to stare with wide eyes at the man who covered Beram.

'Not so fast, my friend,' said a cool voice, as Rustom dexterously snatched the revolver from the man's grasp.

The disarmed newcomer ducked and did a swift somersault, butting his head into Rustom and then coming to grips with him. Taking his cue, Tinker sprang onto Beram's back and held his neck in a vice-like grip, with his legs entwined round his waist in a cruel leg lock. But taking advantage of Tinker's weakened condition, Beram dashed the lad against the wall, where he fell in a huddled heap.

Rid of his burden, Beram lent a hand to Rustom to capture the man he believed to be his nemesis.

Chapter XXXIX

It was 9 o'clock in the morning in Poona, on the one-year anniversary of the photograph of the grim secrets lying at the bottom of the Tower of Silence.

Nothing was visible from the outside of the structure that morning, except the circular wall that rose twenty feet high. On the trees and on the edges of the walls were perched a number of vultures. Their appearance, with their long necks and hooked beaks, was a sight that caused a shiver to run down the spines of even those accustomed to the sight, and a nameless fright to those foreign to the creed of Zoroaster.

A small procession was coming up the steps leading towards the dokhma. In the lead was a man whose duty it was to see that the road was clear. Just behind him were four coffin bearers supporting a weight on their shoulders. Four others in pairs walked on either side of the coffin holding two ends of tapes passed over the corpse. When the coffin bearers tired, these four extra men were ready to relieve them. After them came the priests, followed by a small band of relatives, friends and acquaintances, walking in pairs, holding two ends of a cloth between them.

The procession did not presume to have any military attitude. There was unity in one sense, however, to compensate for maintaining regular footsteps in tune to music, and that was in the subdued heads and bent shoulders of mourning.

There was no music because Zoroastrians relate music purely to happy occasions and believe its presence at so sorrowful a time a hindrance to deep thoughts and prayers for the dead. These are murmured all the way from the house of the deceased to the final resting place. The mourners, including the coffin bearers, were all dressed in white. White is the fashion in wedding ceremonies for Zoroastrians too. A deep philosophy underlies this anomaly, which is that white is the colour of purity. Dirt cannot be concealed on white clothing whereas a coloured garment may be worn many times over and still look presentable.

The procession threaded its way to the gate of the enclosure. The coffin was gently laid on the ground. The part of the sheet covering the face was removed for the gathering to have one last look before it was covered up again. The coffin was then lifted and taken through the gates on the shoulders of four bearers. The mourners prayed near the fire temple until a signal was given that the uncovered corpse had been placed in a furrow in the well wall, ready to be devoured by the vultures.

In this instance, the corpse was not placed in the regular Tower of Silence, where all true believers were laid to rest, but was left in a smaller structure, specially set apart for thieves, murderers, converts and other questionable elements.

As the reader must have guessed, the body deposited in the smaller tower was none other than that of Young. It was he who was stripped naked, and with bound hands and feet and a gag in his mouth, was left on his back, at the total mercy of the birds of prey.

When the coffin was put down before the gates, and his face was exposed to the gaze of all, Young seemed to all intents and purposes quite dead. However, to leave him to the vultures after he was dead could scarcely give satisfaction to the outraged religious sensibilities of his captors. A more terrible end awaited the aviator who had taken the forbidden photograph, either for money or because he believed he could do things with impunity because he was British.

A specially prepared serum had been injected into his body. This paralyzed him, yet his senses remained perfectly alert and active. His eyes were purposely kept open, so that though he could not move the lids, yet he could distinctly see things and register them in his brain. No sooner had they laid him down, than one of the coffin secured eye glasses over his eyes. Then he removed a syringe from his pocket and injected it into the nape of Young's neck.

Once he was abandoned, the vultures closed in around him, but kept their distance when they sensed this was a living being. An hour passed with Young in sheer terror, in expectation of his flesh being ripped open by a daring bird among the flock. Once it began, the end would not be long in coming. But just when Young thought the patience of the vultures must be at an end, he was saved by a fresh arrival.

Once again, the same coffin bearers brought another burden and deposited it in another furrow, a yard away from Young. By turning his head, Young saw that it was none other then Stephens who was being administered an injection. As Stephens regained consciousness, the two men helped ward off the birds by moving constantly, writhing, twisting, raising up their legs or their elbows or heads in any number of ways.

But they had to keep up these fatiguing movements. When the sun reached its height, they knew that sooner or later, their movements would cease through sheer exhaustion. At that point, the birds would not hesitate. An hour later, they were joined by the Baron, followed by Martin and finally Tinker.

It was past noon and the sun was merciless in its intensity. Save for Tinker, the men had slipped closer to the mouth of the well in the centre. They were in danger of falling in, the sloping wall of the structure being purposely constructed to allow the bones of consumed bodies to slip into the hollow vault.

Young's position was most precarious. His feet were dangling over the precipice and he was forced to stay still, counting upon his neighbours on either side to drive away a daring bird. Only Tinker had a peak cap placed on his head, which protected the upper half of his face from the killing rays of the sun. He was also not gagged as the others were, and it was he who warned Young of his precarious position and advised him not to move at all.

At first, Tinker cried out for help lustily, but after an hour of shouting, his voice fell to a hoarse, scarcely audible whisper, hissing through his parched throat.

Chapter XL

'Come in, Mr Blake,' Beram murmured languidly as he sat on a specially designed, low easy chair.

Blake, who had just peeped out from a secret door in the wall of the room, was taken aback at the invitation. He had assumed himself undetected. Walking out of his hiding place, he stood grimly facing Beram.

'Please sit down. It's a bit awkward having you standing there while I'm lounging around.' Beram drawled, without making any move to stand up.

'Beram at your service,' purred the mastermind, who had successfully conducted his mission.

'Don't be so sure about yourself, my slippery friend. Between myself and Bonzo here, I think you are sunk,' Blake said pointing to the police bloodhound at his heels. 'In fact, I challenge you to make good your escape.'

'If I were you, I would not depend too much upon Bonzo. I can strike him lifeless with a single glance. As for your revolver, I wager you the freedom of all your friends against my voluntary captivity that you would not dare to fire it at me, even if I were to get up and coolly walk away from here. In fact, I am tempted to do so, if it were not for the fact that it does not suit my purpose at the moment.'

'What makes you think I would not dare? If you think your eastern tricks will make me miss my mark, you are mistaken.'

'The first reason you dare not fire is that you will find yourself in a hornet's nest when my followers learn of my death. You would live for only a few moments.'

'What if I have a silencer attached to my piece?'

'You have not heard me give you the second reason.'

'Well?'

'If you fire and your shot proves fatal, my followers will make short shrift of our prisoners.'

'Oh, is that so? Come out, Melley, and hold this customer on point, will you? And if it comes to that, don't hesitate to shoot. And shoot to kill. No half measures. As to rescuing my friends, I am willing to take the chance and find them without your learned guidance.'

'As you wish,' murmured Beram.

Here, a little elucidation is necessary. Beram, as we know, did not expect Blake to appear in so abrupt a manner. To his credit, though, he sensed his presence in Bombay. It was the reason he used the bait of the scent at the inquest. But Blake did not respond to the bait and Beram had assumed himself to be wrong. Despite his disadvantage at being taken by surprise, he had not lost his nerve. Instead, he concentrated and sent a telepathic message to Rustom who was in a house a short distance away.

'Come, Rustom, come here at once. Come, come,

come here. Rustom, Rustom, do you hear me? Come, come, come by the secret passage. Danger ahead, Rustom. Rustom, do you hear me? Come-come-come here at once.'

Rustom had felt quite at a loss to comprehend the curious state of his mind. Resting his head against the back of a chair, he wondered what had come over him. It was then that he had heard Beram's message, as clear as the chimes of a bell. After having tuned himself to a receptive mood, he prepared himself to send a message in reply.

'Coming, master, coming—coming, coming,coming.'

'Overcome the other, but leave Blake to me,' Beram responded.

Rustom had sprung to his feet and raced to a desk. He grabbed a revolver from the drawer and put it in his right pocket. In his bedroom, he pulled on a pair of specially made rubber-soled shoes that were soundless. He then crawled under the bed, opened a concealed trap door, and disappeared inside. Using the network of underground passageways, he was soon at the opening leading to Beram's room.

From his hidden position, he could see a line of policeman standing so close that they were almost touching each other, with revolvers ready in their hands. With barely time to think, he had made an audacious plan. He lunged at the last man in the line with a blow that stunned him. The young policeman went rigid and fell against the man beside him. In short order, all the policemen were knocked off their feet and lay spread about the floor.

Rustom stepped over the uniformed men but stopped in his tracks when he saw Blake standing with a revolver pointing straight to his heart. He also saw Bonzo, the large bloodhound, crouching near Beram, ready to spring upon him if he made the slightest move. At that moment, Blake opened the safe in the corner of the room with the key he had taken from Beram.

'Here is evidence enough to hang you, my friend.' Blake said when he saw the personal effects of his friends. Removing a small glass jar, he took it out and shook it. 'What in the name of thunder is this?'

'Preserves.'

'In a safe?'

'Pass me a piece and help yourself to a slice, if you are not afraid of eating it.'

CHAPTER XLI

Rustom saw the commissioner positioned opposite the door, almost in the centre of the room. He was standing guard with his revolver pointed at Beram, with Bonzo the bloodhound at his feet. The last time Rustom had come to Beram's aid, they had been in Bombay. They had escaped from the clutches of Blake and the police after recapturing all their prisoners and moving them to another safe location in Poona.

Rustom was a man of action rather than a thinker, which was why he had been appointed second in command. Beram was the mastermind, the weaver of the web, but his plans would fall flat if they were not executed by a fearless follower. This is not to say that Rustom was lacking in thought. Having decided on a course of action, in a trice, Rustom pulled out his silenced revolver and fired a shot.

Wizz!

The bullet struck square at the pistol held by Melley.

The silenced shot caused the bewildered commissioner no end of surprise. Nor was Blake prepared for what followed. As the pistol fell from Melley's hand, Beram became a seething mass of energy. He shot a quick jab at the pit of Blake's stomach and launched himself off the chair. By the impetus he thus received, he took a backward somersault and landed on the windowsill. The next second, he had vanished.

In the moment of Beram's manoeuvre, Bonzo rushed at Rustom with the speed of an arrow. The object of his fury would have suffered severely from the savage attack had not Rustom stepped out of the way, causing the dog to skid into the passage whereupon Rustom banged the door shut.

'Hands up,' Rustom roared at Melley.

Still gasping from Beram's blow but seeing Melley's predicament, Blake gave the agreed upon signal to the policemen gathered outside. But nothing came of it. Lying on the ground with his hand pressed tightly over his stomach, Blake contorted his face in pain as he removed a pistol tucked under his belt. When he took his shot he intended for the bullet to strike Rustom's right hand, but it struck his thigh instead, passing through his flesh and instantly dying his white flannel pants with blood.

Rustom, with great willpower, tried to ignore the wound. Determined not to let Beram escape, Blake made a cat-like spring to the windowsill, through which he too disappeared from view. Blake's shot had another unintended consequence when another figure, a soldier in Beram's squad responding to the noise, came stealthily into the room and rushed Melley from behind. The Englishman was soon secured in true professional style, the handcuffs in his own pocket serving the purpose.

CHAPTER XLII

The house from which Beram so dramatically escaped was situated in a valley between two hills, one high and seemingly inaccessible, and the other comparatively low. When Blake tumbled out of the window, Beram was already a fair distance away, running at topmost speed towards the higher hill. Blake, nothing loath, broke into a sprint and pursued him.

Blake was an athlete and, in spite of his advanced age, he was in full form, but he quickly discerned that he had met his match. The regular though fast pace that Beram maintained showed great strength, agility and endurance. The easy, measured stride, the erect poise of the body and the perfect rhythm all carried a depressing message to Blake that the only chance he had of catching Beram would be luck or by tearing every sinew of every muscle in his body.

Beram led his adversary to the top of the hill and then descended on the other side, his object being to tire out his pursuer. When Blake reached the summit, he saw that the incline was smooth and richly covered with grass. To increase his speed, he feverishly tore off his coat, wrapped it around his head, fell upon the ground with his arms tucked rigidly to his side and began to roll down the hill.

When Beram glanced behind him, he did not see the detective. Thinking Blake must have given up the chase, he stopped running.

Suddenly, Beram felt something bump hard against his legs, almost knocking him down. The tall grass had effectively concealed Blake during his tumbling descent. Beram sprinted away like a hunted deer before Blake could regain his feet and catch hold of him.

Only thirty yards now separated the two men. The tumbling descent had given Blake a brief period of rest that had been denied to Beram. This counted much in his favour, and he now managed to close the distance to fifteen yards.

So on they ran, the hound and the hare, at a pace that a professional might envy. Blake's only thoughts were of his friends and of his assistant. The object of his pursuit, the man who could help him free his comrades, was displaying great agility and Blake feared he might slip between his fingers.

But there's many a slip betwixt the cup and the lip. Slowly, but surely, by inches, the distance between them decreased. Blake gave an additional spurt like a sprinter close to the finish line. Now he was barely three yards away. It seemed that in the very next minute Blake would lay his outstretched hand upon his adversary's shoulder. But when Beram felt Blake's hot gasping breath on the nape of his neck, he stopped dead in his tracks and fell upon the ground crosswise, with one leg stretched straight and stiff across Blake's path.

The fall would not have been so severe if not for the great momentum Blake's speed had built. Blake flew high up in the air and fell at a distance of five yards from the place of contact. Blake was momentarily dazed while Beram quietly squatted on his haunches, the fingertips of his hands resting on the ground.

Blake's mind was confused after the fall. Seeing Beram's posture, Blake believed Beram was on the point of dashing away. With superhuman effort, he rose and rushed towards him, planning to use a fatal ju-jitsu move that he had learned in Argentina, the effects of which he had never dared to try until now. But desperate times called for desperate measures.

When Blake rushed upon him, Beram shot up from his crouch like a catapult and threw his right shoulder with such dexterity, force and speed into Blake's chest that the latter fell with a gasp at his feet. But Beram did not take advantage of the former's helplessness, knowing such an act would be devoid of all sense of fair play and decency.

CHAPTER XLIII

'H-e-l-p-p-p,' Tinker managed to shout out one last time, before he fell mute from exhaustion.

Physically weakened by the unbearable heat of the sun, his thoughts grew confused. The stone around him was like a furnace. The situation was intolerable. When Tinker turned his head, the sight that greeted his eyes made his heart leap into his mouth.

With his legs dangling over the brink of the well, Stephens was jerking his body unconsciously. It was indeed a mercy that Beram had not ordered the victims to be stripped naked. Otherwise, they would never have escaped the cruel beaks of the ruthless vultures. Tinker agitatedly warned him not to move an inch further, but to no avail. The man was half mad from the heat.

At this juncture, fate intervened. One of the vultures approached Young, and catching hold of his clothes above his shoulders, furiously tugged at him in a determined endeavour to drag him back to safety. Though the bird was large, its attempts proved futile, and the effect it produced was to send a chill of terror into Young's heart. Tinker saw what the bird was attempting to do, and comprehending its motives, warned Stephens and the Baron not to disturb it. Seeing their mate's attempts to save their dinner from falling into the pit, two or three other birds boldly hopped closer. Their united efforts succeeded in dragging Young a foot or two away from the danger zone.

What with Tinker's hullaballoo and the raising of the legs and hands of the others, and the jerks of Young's head, the birds were once again scared away. They flew a few yards away and sat there with exemplary patience.

Young was now lost to the world and totally unconscious when all of a sudden and without any warning, a daring bird suddenly came and perched upon the breast of the aviator. He was hardly seated before he pecked viciously at the goggles tied over Young's eyes. Although it had not succeeded, the bird persisted to strike at the goggles, as it is the instinct of this species to first attack the eyes. It was an instinct that saved Young's face from being terribly mutilated.

Tinker screamed with terror. But neither his voice, nor the desperate attempts of both Stephens and the Baron to frighten the bird away were of any account.

Just as the other birds were emboldened by this courageous move, a deftly thrown stone struck the head of the bird perched on Young with such force that it writhed on the ground in a mad endeavour before plunging over the brink of the wall in a wild flutter, after spattering no small amount of blood on the clothes of the unconscious Englishman. The fate of their comrade frightened the birds clustered round the victims so much that all of them took to their wings and flew towards the neighbouring trees.

Meanwhile, a curious drama was being enacted on the wall of the Tower of Silence. At the very moment when the vulture had been furiously pecking at Young's eyes, a man had crept up on his stomach along the pathway taken by the corpse bearers. His aim was to approach the victims stealthily, cut their bonds and then help them to escape. But the unfortunate moment when the bird took into its head to attack the aviator spoiled his plan. Submitting to the exigency of the moment, he had to throw the stone at the bird to save Young's life.

Unfortunately, this manoeuvre required standing up. He was then spotted by Beram's men. Three stalwart individuals fell in a heap upon him and managed to secure him after a short struggle.

Chapter XLIV

Blake anxiously began to scrutinize the plain, trying to spot Beram, when he heard him speak.

'Now listen, Mr Blake, I assure you, I will not attempt to escape. When you have caught your breath, I am willing to fight the matter out in any way you like.'

At this, Blake's cheek flushed hot, but he pocketed his pride. The battle of wits had been fought long and hard. Now the final test remained of their respective individual physical strength and powers of endurance.

After an interval of five minutes, Blake was ready. Though he was sorely tempted to launch a surprise attack, the fairness shown towards him by Beram made him give fair warning to his adversary.

'Are you ready?'

'When was I not!' drawled Beram as he jumped to his feet.

'Come on then. Do you intend to stand and fight it out like a man or sprint away like a dancing girl?'

'That taunt is unwarranted. I could have shown you a clean pair of heels long ago.'

Blake advanced towards his man until he was within striking range.

'Wait. Would you not like to come on firmer ground?'

'My dear sir, I am a very busy man. I prefer to finish the matter here and now.'

'What's it to be? Wrestling or—'

'No need to stand on any ceremony, my scrupulous friend. Let it be a rough and tumble and hit where you please. There is no referee to watch over the niceties.'

Both instinctively took up a boxing stance. Blake levelled a straight left on the jaw. It missed slightly, landing on Beram's neck. As he staggered back, Blake followed it up with a right hand punch that landed on Beram's chest, making the Parsee fall on his back.

'One, two ….' Blake began counting when Beram jumped up and slipped a clean cut under Blake's guard, while swinging out his right leg with a jerk just behind Blake's knee joint. Blake lost his balance. But the result was quite unexpected. Beram slipped and fell first, right in the path of Blake. It was lucky for Beram that he had fallen upon all fours, thus receiving Blake on his back or he would have been pinned below his adversary.

Blake passed his left arm below Beram's chin and turned it to the left. At the same time, he clutched a clump of his hair and yanked it to the right, all the while holding Beram's waist in a scissor grip. Beram's arms sagged and he fell flat on the ground on his chin. Beram raised his legs and swung them high in the air. Though encumbered with the legs of the detective twirled round his waist like fast-clinging ivy, he performed a neat semicircle over Blake's head.

Beram applied pressure on a nerve that half paralyzed Blake's arm. He immediately loosened his grip. They tumbled about in a close embrace. The pain they inflicted upon each other was so great, and the torture experienced by them individually was so exquisite, that both of them let go of the hold and simultaneously sprang to their feet, undecided about how to continue.

'Truce for ten minutes,' Beram gasped.

'If you promise not to run away.'

CHAPTER XLV

'Hope you feel easy now, my friend,' Beram said, resting on the ground.

'Oh, quite,' replied Blake. 'Now look here, Mr…'

'Beram. You can call me Beram.'

'Beram, from what little I know of you, I don't think you are as bad as all that.'

'I too admire you, Mr Blake'

'The Parsee community, to which you belong, is well-known for practising the Western principles of fair play and chivalry.'

'Flattery will scarcely avail you, my dear sir.'

'There is nothing more contemptible than to praise an ill-deserving person. But can we not come to some terms?'

'My cause is sacred and just. Do not think for a moment, that it is an outcome of the blind faith of the zealot. The reason for my actions is plain, based on equity and justice and high ethical principles. These principles will stand up to any test of logic.'

Though Blake was burning with impatience to reach his friends, he had to humour the man. He knew that to expose non-Parsees on the Tower of Silence entailed great risks for the perpetrators. The notice given to Stephens at his London office warning him of what lay in store might have lead them to suppose that the authorities in Poona would have prepared a reception. Thus it was more likely that the captives had been taken to a tower other than the one photographed, one unknown to Blake.

'But what is the harm if a photo is taken?' Blake asked.

Before answering, Beram had a long and steady look through his binoculars at a smaller hill some good distance away. What he saw made him blanche, but he collected himself and replied to Blake.

'Now listen to me attentively. There is scarcely any time to lose. Your friends have been lying exposed to the sun for the last four hours. It is merciful providence that the vultures have not made short shrift of them as yet. You ask me what harm there is if a photo is taken? You may see none. But you forget the ethical principles on which our religion is based. Purity is everything to our religion. Purity from all points of view, not just bodily purity. Animals can achieve bodily purity. Even a pig can be outwardly clean. For us, there must also be purity of actions. Of course no one is perfect.'

At this stage, Blake's impatience can be better imagined than described. Blake's thoughts were centred entirely upon the state of his friends. When he heard that they had already been taken to the Tower of Silence and had been lying exposed there for hours, he was even more distressed. He felt like reaching out and strangling Beram, but restrained himself.

'A bad action of a member of our community is something that has to be dealt with or purged altogether. When the tips of our fingers or nose rot, do we cut them away altogether? No. The individuals are the limbs of the community. This is not a case of "what cannot be mended should be ended". To the contrary, it is the contradiction of that maxim.'

'We are very zealous in guarding our purity from foreign influence. By foreign influence, I mean not only those that are apart and distinct from our religion, but also that which cannot be seen, heard or felt, but which nevertheless exists. In the light of our present-day knowledge and advancement in various branches of learning, we are now quite cognizant of the power our thoughts are capable of. What was formerly blindly believed is now based on our firm conviction garbed in the cloak of reason. We now know what it is that makes one mind dominate another, or dominate a crowd of other minds.

'Similarly the influence of the eye. An eye is the direct channel through which the mind is influenced. The evil influence of the eye was well-guarded against in old times. An evil eye may wither a child, as time and exposure does a flower. This brought out the creation of charms to guard children against such evil influences. Much depends on the eye's influence. That's why Hindus do not sit in the presence of low castes, and never allow their children to do so. Similarly, I may remark en passant, that a passionate eye is the bane of beauty.

'We now know that hypnotism is a force that has come to stay. There is no doubt that even an average man has latent mesmeric powers. It is generally the case that the mind is influenced through the medium of the eyes. Even when the mind determines to influence a distant object, it must visualize the object. It is this purity, namely the evil influence of the eye, against which our main religious contention is based. The photograph broke one of the principle tenets of our faith. As a consequence, your friends are undergoing insufferable torture.'

Blake winced.

'A foreign eye, accompanied by evil thoughts, has peered into the sacred repository of the dead. No foreign eye should fall upon the sacred precincts of our temples or our towers. The very atmosphere of the universe, surcharged almost electrically by the chantings of never-ceasing prayers, which is built like a cordon around our places of worship, has been disturbed.

'That's why we zealously guard against any intrusion. In fact, we would not mind a person coming in close proximity to the sacred precincts of our temples blindfolded. It is the eye that is the root cause of all evil. Of course, the eye of a child or that of a saintly person may be tolerated.'

Blake nodded.

'When I speak of the eye's influence, I speak of facts and solid realities and not a chimera of the mind. It is no fantasy. It is the eye that is the source of impurity. It is the eye that turns heaven into hell and vice versa.'

'I see, I see,' said Blake, hoping he was done.

'I believe that no amount of harshness towards your friends can effectively remedy the present evil and prevent others treading the same path they have taken. I feel it will better benefit our cause if we allow them to live after the soul-wracking experience they have received.'

'Yes, yes,' Blake breathed anxiously, temporarily blinded by the big drops of perspiration rolling down his forehead and into his eyes. 'I will undertake to broadcast your views in England in such a manner that in future no one will think of ever crossing the limits of good sense and discretion. I think I can even influence my government to pass a ban upon all such adventures.'

'I believe every word that you say,' Beram said. Then giving Blake the binoculars, he pointed to a small hill. 'Look. That is where they are. They are exposed on the Chotra, not on the regular Tower of Silence.'

CHAPTER XLVI

'Good God,' Blake said, once his eyes discerned the sight. Horror was depicted on every line of his face, mixed with fury at the originator of the deed. He felt as if he were suffocating and indeed took breaths in big gasps, as if the very air had been denied to him. Nevertheless, he had sufficient presence of mind not to offend Beram.

He threw his jacket on the ground and took off at top speed for the neighbouring hill.

'Stop, stop,' thundered Beram. 'You rush to your destruction.'

Blake had no ears but for his own laboured breath. No eyes but for the scene that had been depicted before him a moment ago. The utter helplessness of his friends gave him the impetus to run. Off he went, pursued by Beram.

Blake was not a man who frightened easily but seeing the bird viciously pecking at the eyes of the inert figure made him lose balance. The tables had turned. The pursued had turned into the pursuer. At last, making a special effort, Beram managed to clutch at the sleeve of Blake's shirt. The action so infuriated Blake that he instantaneously turned round and smashed Beram's nose.

Blake had already gone quite some distance before Beram started again in dogged pursuit, determined to stop him. Beram drew nearer but decided to run past Blake and obtrude his way from the front. Once he was past Blake, he kept on running faster to increase his lead as much as possible. He turned and stood his ground only when he was two yards ahead. With the spring of an acrobat, Beram threw himself on Blake, entwining his arms around him.

Blake managed to shake him off and began punching Beram. But while Beram ducked and fended off his blows, he did not return anything in kind. Finally, Beram caught hold of Blake's right wrist and, twisting his arm around his back, brought him down on the ground.

Chapter XLVII

'For heaven's sake, man, listen. Or everything will be lost,' whispered Beram. 'We are being observed by my associates, whose one aim in life is to take revenge for the wrong done to us. Whereas I look into the future and think it more judicious and fruitful to let your friends live.'

'Wait!' he hissed, as Blake became impatient at this untimely lecture. 'You will reach there more quickly by tarrying here awhile. After two minutes, make a run for the hill. If you are successful in reaching there, you will not be molested while trying to free your friends. But there is one barrier you will have to overcome. If you are faced with a wall of flames, don't dare to pass through it, for it will surely consume you as it is of a degree sufficient to melt solid iron in thirty seconds.'

Blake looked at him in a bewildered manner.

'I will take the lead and you follow, pretending to catch me.' Beram said as he took off, Blake hard on his heels.

They had reached the base of the hill where the captives were confined, when all of a sudden, there arose before them a five-foot high wall of flames.

'To attempt to pass through this is to court certain death. But I will make it subside.'

No sooner had Beram said this than he took out a tight fitting skull-cap of white mulmul from his pocket and fixed it on his head. He then lifted up his shirt front, and tucking it under his chin, unwound his kusti, from around his waist and retied it, musically chanting all the while.

Murmuring other hymns, he forged his way through the flames.

Blake saw Beram run crosswise, instead of straight at the hill. He hesitated for a minute and had just decided to take the plunge when something fell from his coat pocket. It was a gunmetal watch with a long chain, gifted to him by a grateful client. He held the free end of the chain in his right hand and approached the live flames, going as close as he dared.

He let the watch swing through just for a brief moment. The effect was that he immediately let it fall. The chain had burned his hand.

'What magical powers these prayers must contain, to control the most independent and destructive element in such a manner!' Blake wondered. Even as the thought passed through his mind, the flames subsided and died away.

Blake veritably flew like something demented towards his objective.

Chapter XLVIII

'Twit – twi – twi – twi – twiiiiii,' came a bird-like signal.

'Twit – twi – twi – twi – twiiiiii,' Blake responded.

'Hoot, hoot,' came the answering signal at last.

But no sooner had he received the answering call then he became aware of a living death sprung up, as it were, from the ground. There wriggled past him, between his right foot and a large stone lying nearby, a long sandh, a very dangerous fifteen-foot reptile. It was a species found in the dense jungles of India. Its sting was not fatal. Instead, it carried death in the strength of its tail. It could kill a man with three strikes of its tail and bring an ox to the ground with a dozen.

Blake saw it just as it wriggled past. Believing that the best course was to let it go unmolested, he watched it slither away. But then the reptile curled itself around an invisible nucleus. It shot up erect on its head and remained momentarily suspended like an overgrown staple of rice. This pose was almost instantaneously converted into a swinging motion. It was now literally skipping on its head to within striking distance of Blake.

With a noise like that of a whiperack, it lashed its tail straight at Blake's shoulders with staggering force.

The surprised detective had no time to understand its manoeuvre. The lash was so sudden and swift that it almost tore open the skin on his back. Once he knew how the creature would attack, Blake was ready for it.

Blake knew it was as dangerous at close quarters as it was at a distance, nevertheless he chose the lesser evil and decided to rush upon it. But just as he decided to take his chance, he was surprised to see the snake shudder, after which it became limp and fell in a crumpled heap. Thinking it a ruse practised by the creature to induce him to come near, Blake fought away from it. He did not see a person move rapidly away and was unaware that the snake had been killed by sheer concentration of someone's mind.

Giving the limp reptile a wide berth, he continued on his way up without any further mishap. Reaching the top, he looked over the wall of the Tower and received a shock.

'Help!' a feeble voice cried out.

Blake recognized the voice as that of his assistant. He did not think it judicious to betray his presence to others before observing the lay of the land, but risked one more look. There Tinker lay. His head was bent a little sideways, as if conscious of Blake's presence. The vultures appeared to be preparing for another attack. When Blake turned his attention to the other helpless forms, he saw that the Baron and Stephens were both in imminent danger of disappearing into the well.

Before he started towards Tinker, three people rushed upon the scene, two in the direction of the Baron and Stephens, while the third ran towards Young. Blake rushed to Tinker and immediately took charge of him. He lifted him bodily and ran towards the shelter afforded by a stand of trees.

One of the rescuers untied a parcel he had carried on his back and took out four soft Parsee silk suits. Throwing one to each of the rescued men, he began to help dress Young. Then flinging him on his shoulders, he raced towards the place where a group of Parsees were washing their hands and faces with water from the big chatties.

'Side, side,' thundered the man bearing Young, closely followed by the three others carrying their burdens upon their shoulders.

'Case of snake bite,' Blake explained to the crowd.

One of the rescuers was a doctor and between him and Blake, they managed to revive the four victims. They were carried to a large motor van to be driven at great speed to the bungalow of the Commissioner of Police. The van had scarcely covered a dozen yards when they heard the roars and shouts of the enraged mob running after them.

'Somehow or the other, they know,' Blake said to himself.

ACKNOWLEDGMENTS

I am deeply grateful to the following who have provided advice, looked up files, offered contacts, and shared my quest for Mr Chaiwala: Muncherji Cama, Peter D'Costa, Cyrus Guzder, Shekhar Krishnan, Chris Moffat, Shehernaz Nalwalla, Nikhil Rao, Vyjanthi Rao, Mitra Sharafi and Dan Sheffield. I am thankful to Aruna Gill, who meticulously copyedited the manuscript, removing repetitions, errors and inconsistencies and ensuring that the narrative flowed crisply while retaining the flavour of Mr Chaiwala's language and style. Thanks are also due to V.K. Karthika of HarperCollins for appreciating the value of the unpublished novel and for making sure that it saw the light of day.